Carry On Henry

The wickedly funny story that
starts where the film ends

Norman Giller

Chameleon

For John East-Here, Terry and Sylvia
Carry On laughing

First published in Great Britain in 1996 by
Chameleon Books
106 Great Russell Street
London WC1B 3LJ

CIP data for this title is available
from the British Library

ISBN 0 233 99032 1

Typeset by Falcon Oast Graphic Art

Printed in Great Britain by WBC, Bridgend

Author's Acknowledgements

This book could not have been written without the original foundation work of *Carry On* film creators Peter Rogers and Gerald Thomas. I have simply carried on where they left off, but I would not even have managed the first step without their marathon screen productions to inspire me. I am also indebted to the *Carry On* team of actors, who brought their characters to life on screen and turned the film series into a national institution. I acknowledge, too, the lovingly crafted screenplays of the writers, and in particular Talbot Rothwell and Norman Hudis. On behalf of the Publishers, I thank the Rank Organisation for allowing us to step into the *Carry On* territory that has always been exclusive to the silver screen, and for their permission to use still photographs from the original film version of *Carry On Henry*.

My thanks also to VCI Chief Executive Steve Ayres for letting me off the leash, and to Tim Forrester, Tom Rosenthal and John Cleary at Chameleon Books for their encouragement; also to my House Editor Stephanie Goodwin, and to Richard Percy, who first had the brainwave to turn the *Carry On* films into books. Most of all, thanks to Eileenalanna, Lisa and Michael for being there.

The characters and events depicted on the following pages are entirely fictitious, and anybody who wishes to argue otherwise will be laughed out of court. *Carry On Laughing...*

The author makes his humblest and heart-felt apologies to The Master, William Shakespeare, for some of the lines you are about to read. But this should not save him from a trip to The Tower. As King Henry would say, 'Off with his head!'

Introduction

This book carries on where the film *Carry On Henry**
left off. The story so far:

The life and times of Henry VIII were chronicled for
the film by court historian William Cobbler, and so the
facts and deeds are accurately described as a load of old
Cobbler's. King Henry (Sidney James) has one wife
beheaded and, within minutes of her head landing in
the basket, he marries Queen Marie (Joan Sims), cousin
of the King of France. Both the execution rites and the
marriage ceremony are conducted by the cunning,
conniving Cardinal Wolsey (Terry Scott). The marriage
has been arranged by Wolsey and the treacherous
Thomas Cromwell (Kenneth Williams) for a randy king
who is interested only in getting his chopper out.

Queen Marie smells so strongly of garlic that Henry
demands a divorce within five minutes of climbing into
the marital bed. Instead he wants to marry the far more
attractive and voluptuous Bettina (Barbara Windsor),
the Earl of Bristol's daughter. It is left to the king's
personal equerry Sir Roger de Lodgerley (Charles

*The classic comedy film *Carry On Henry* is available in the *Carry
On* series on Cinema Club videos, distributed by VCI, price £4.99.

Hawtrey) to keep Queen Marie happy in bed, while Lord Hampton of Wick plots to overthrow Henry with the help of explosives expert Guy Fawkes (Bill Maynard). Henry survives the gunpowder plot when Guy Fawkes succeeds in blowing up only himself.

Francis I, King of France (Peter Gilmore), arrives in England to visit his cousin, and Queen Marie is released from the Tower to greet him. King Francis is delighted to find that she is expecting, which is most unexpected by Henry because he has yet to consummate the marriage. Henry loses Bettina to the handsome, dashing King Francis, and, to save face, has to acknowledge that the baby – the image of soppy Sir Roger – is his son and heir.

Our story starts with Henry still desperate to get out of his marriage to Queen Marie. His roving eye has now been taken by buxom serving wench Nell Grinn, who bears a striking resemblance to Barbara Windsor. Queen Marie is in no mood to let her 'Enri go, and sets out to humiliate her husband. He would like to order her head to be chopped off, but he fears that the public would turn against him. Marie has won her way into their hearts, and his loyal subjects think they have an idyllic marriage.

Bernard Bresslaw's lookalike makes an entry into our story as the king's advisor Bernardo, who keeps Henry informed by taking out his glass eye and looking into the future. It's a future clouded with problems for Henry. Has his chopper at last been blunted? Luckily for historians Will the Quill, or Will the Winker as he is known to his friends (and looking for all the world and its stage like Kenneth Connor), is on hand to keep a record of events.

Now it's on with the codpieces, the breeches and the silk hose (and this is for the men) for an hysterical rather than historical trip back into Britain's past. *Carry On reading...*

1

NELL GRINN, a buxom serving wench at the Peacock and Partridge inn, slapped the hand of the customer whose gnarled hand had wandered from his tankard to her shapely bottom. 'Kindly keep thy hands to thyself, sire,' she said, 'or I will tell the landlord to kick thee in thy breeches.'

The customer chortled. 'I like thy spirit, wench,' he said, reaching for the pear that rested on her tray. 'What say I walketh thee home, and that we hath some nibbles together?'

Nell was accustomed to these sort of advances, and gave him the stock answer. 'Go stuffeth thyself,' she said.

That made the customer laugh all the more. 'Thou slayeth me,' he said, his podgy fingers now pinching the pert bottom covered by an ankle-length skirt and half a dozen underskirts.

Nobody did that to Nell Grinn uninvited. Her right hand was a blur as she cuffed the man across his black whiskered face. She was astonished to find the whiskers fly from his ruddy cheeks into his tankard of beer. Now a reddish-brown beard was revealed.

The landlord, Lemmie Pulham, came over to see what the commotion was about. 'Dangle my donglers, what occureth here?' he said sternly, then suddenly dropped down on one knee.

'What the bleedin' 'ell is up with thee?' asked Nell.

'Hath thou been imbibing to excess again?'

'Thy Majesty!' said Pulham to the hugely wide man filling the chair in front of him. ''Tis an honour to hath thou gracing us with thy presence.'

Nell dropped her wooden serving tray in shock, and gave a deep curtsy and a full eyeful of her overflowing assets.

King Henry VIII, for it was he, beckoned them both to get up, although he would have preferred Nell to stay down. 'Please, prithee, let us have no fuss,' he pleaded. 'I am here incognito.'

'In where?' said Nelly. 'This is the Peacock and Partridge in Richmond, Surrey, Thy Majesty.'

'Yea, I knoweth that,' said the king. 'My abode is just down the road at Hampton Court. This is my third night here on what are purely discreet private visits. Nobody is to knoweth of my presenth... I mean, presence.'

'Anything thou commandeth,' said Pulham bowing and vowing. 'May my lips be torn from my mouth and fed to the foxes if I breathe a word to a living soul, nay, or even to the ghosts of the graveyard.'

No such vow was made by Claude de Bedsop, a French undercover agent who was a master of deception and disguise. He was hidden in the corner of the inn, looking for all the world like a barrel of ale. Claude the Fraud, as he was known within the French secret service, had been assigned to trail the king by Henry's wife, Marie, Queen of England and second in line to the French throne, who suspected him of getting his royal leg over. So far Bedsop had evidence only of him looking but not touching.

Claude, an expert on matters of *l'amour*, sensed *le touche* was imminent.

'How canst I, thy humblest of servants, be of service to thee, my liege?' asked Pulham.

'It is not thy service I am after, Landlord,' the king said, winking. ''Tis the wench here I am looking to service me, if thou followeth.'

Pulham looked puzzled, but was instantly more understanding when King Henry placed a small purse of gold in his hand. 'This wilt compensate thee for the time thou have to maketh do without the wench whilst she is in my bed... I mean, company.'

The gold was the equivalent of a lifetime's wages. For that, the king could have bought the Peacock and Partridge, and had the pigs, pigeons, parrots and porcupines thrown in.

''Old on a bleedin' minute,' said Nelly, a girl of proud and obstinate nature. 'I'm not a piece of bleedin' meat what thou can sell at any price. Even if thou art the King of England, I'm not a girl of easy virtue. My legs stay crosseth until I meet a man I loveth with all my hearteth... I mean, heart.'

The landlord winced as he imagined her sweet, slender neck with an executioner's axe slicing through it. She had just rebuffed the man known to his subjects behind – and to the left and right of – his exceedingly broad back as Mad King Chopper of Hampton. He nervously felt his own throat as he wondered and worried as to whether he would be considered an accessory to the crime of giving King Henry what was known among the plebeians as the Spanish kiss... the *El Bow*.

'Do not be a silly nilly, Nelly,' hissed the landlord, as the king snatched back his bag of gold. ''Tis thy duty to do thy duty to king and country. Just lie on thy back and think of England.'

'I never lie, whether 'tis on my back or front,' said Nelly, with a defiant toss of her fair head that any executioner would have been proud to have adorning his basket.

The king was visibly shaken. This was the first time in his life that a girl had ever said 'no' to his advances. He had so many notches on his chopper that he was soon going to have to order a new axe. Never had he been so excited by a challenge.

Henry took one gold coin from the bag. 'Here, my man,' he said, handing it to the grasping landlord. 'Let this compensate for the time lost as this wench goeth off early so that I may walketh her home.'

'*This* is my 'ome,' said Nell. 'I hath a cubby hole upstairs.'

'And what sort of a hole doth thou hath downstairs?' said the king with his subtle sense of humour that always triggered great guffaws of laughter at court.

So he was just a little startled by Nelly's response. She cuffed him around the whiskers again, and this time it stung because he did not have a false beard to cushion the blow.

''Ow dare thee, sire,' she said. 'I'm a lady and wisheth to be treated like one.'

The landlord cringed and subconsciously rubbed at his neck. 'I beggeth thy pardon, my liege,' he said, going down on one knee and hiding the gold coin under the mat. 'I have never been able to break this one's spirit since I took her in as a young orphan girl.'

'Let me at least court you,' said Henry, whose heart had been completely stolen by the serving wench. Not only was she spirited and obviously chaste, but she had the biggest, firmest and fruitiest pair of knockers he had ever seen.

'But thy wife will not liketh it,' said Nelly.

'My wife is not going to get it,' said Henry, pulling a face. 'Thou seest, she doth not understand me.'

A frown crossed Nelly's pretty face. 'Oh dear,' she said, sympathetically. 'Why is that, sire?'

'Mainly because she can hardly speak a word of English and my French is double Dutch to her,' said the king.

'But 'ow did thee manage to woo her and win her 'and?' asked Nelly, now sitting on Henry's chubby knee to where she had been pulled by the king and pushed by the landlord, whose beady eye was on the royal purse while the immoral monarch was more interested in a rare pussy.

'I married her for my country,' he said. 'In fact I hath married all of my wives for England's sake. None of them have yet managed to produce what I wisheth above all else.'

'A son and heir, sire?' said Nelly.

'Well that,' said Henry, 'but I was thinking more of an orgasm that maketh the earth move.'

'I know not of what thou speaketh,' said Nelly, with a blush that suggested to Henry that perhaps she was telling a little porkie.

11

'I married Marie only because my advisors Cromwell and the cunning, conniving Wolsey arranged it,' said the king, his hands wandering from Nelly's trim waist towards her warm thighs until slapped and pushed back to whence they had wandered.

'Drang my dingpops, we knoweth Cardinal Wolsey well here at the Peacock and Partridge,' said the landlord, hovering in case the bag of gold was back up for grabs. 'During the five years that he superviseth the building of the palace at Hampton Court he used to call in here every lunchtime for a flagon of wine. Didn't put his hand in his pocket once, the old miser. We were delighted, my liege, when we heardst thou had persuaded him to maketh a gift of Hampton Court to thee.* At least thou wilt pay thy way at the bar.'

Henry gave him another gold coin, and shooed him away. Pulham bowed low, picking up the other coin from beneath the mat, and backed away richer by the equivalent of six months' takings. He would do all in his power to encourage the courtship of Nelly by the man with the golden purse. Nelly, he realised, had a golden pussy. What a lucky day it was twenty-two years earlier when he and his wife found her abandoned on their doorstep in a wicker basket. Tied to her foot was a label that read: FEEDETH ME AND CLOTHETH ME AND ONE DAY I SHALL BRING THEE RICHES BEYOND THY DREAMS.

---

*It took 2,500 construction workers five years to complete the original Hampton Court at a cost of 200,000 gold crowns. It had 1000 rooms, with 280 silken, four-poster beds kept always ready for visitors. In 1525 Cardinal Wolsey, currying favour with the King, presented Hampton Court to him. It was the most extravagant gift ever made by a subject, and it broke Wolsey's heart. He had built the palace for his own use.

Pulham and his wife decided on the name Nell Grinn because Knell was a death bell that they thought might be soon ringing for the sickly-looking child, and Grinn because she was always smiling when they first took her in, mainly because of the wind. Now she had grown into the most beautiful woman in the whole of Surrey, but the riches beyond dreams had yet to follow. Perhaps at last, thought Pulham, the gold was about to flow.

The king resumed talking to Nell and the unseen ears of Claude de Bedsop. 'Cromwell and Wolsey assured me that Marie was both frisky and fertile,' he said, 'but all they were really interested in was getting their fingers into the French treasury, having between them virtually cleaned out the English vaults. For that I have to suffer the insufferable stench of garlic, French toast for breakfast, luncheon and dinner and never so much as a French kiss.'

The barrel of ale tilted as Claude the Fraud made copious notes.

Nelly kissed him lightly on his wide forehead that had a receding hairline, his once bright ginger hair darkening and thinning. 'Thou poor soul,' she said. 'From what we learn from the Thames-side town crier and the *Panorama Times*, I thought this time thou had foundest true love.'

'Never believeth what thou readeth in that rag,' said Henry. 'Marie hath friends on that scandal sheet who printeth what she wants them to printeth. And as for the town crier, he crieth a pack of lies every time he openeth that large mouth of his. He is a disgrace to the BBC, the British Broadcasting Criers. Only last week he was going around shouting that the Queen and I will be attending the Lord Mayor of London's annual ball together. That, if you will forgiveth me sweet Nelly, is a loadeth of balls.'

The cockerel in the corner of the inn crowed six times. 'Hell's bells, Nell, is that the time,' said Henry, suddenly getting up and dropping her unceremoniously on to the floor. 'It's going to be a wrench to leave you wench, but I must away to a meeting of the privy council. They are discussing my request for a trebling of my annual income. Queen Marie spendeth my money as if it is water. She and my sister-in-law, Princess Flirty of Flanders, will bankrupteth me unless I can findeth an excuse for locking them out of harm's way in the Tower.'

'But thy good wife looketh so innocent in her portraits, my Lord,' said Nell, 'and with the most beautiful blue staring eyes.'

'That's that bloody Hans Holbein, the mad painter from Germany,' said Henry. 'I invited him to join my court as official painter so that he could decorateth a few rooms at Hampton Court, and he spendeth all his time painting portraits. The minute I stop moving he's there, brushing away at his canvas. He flattereth all my wives, but portrayeth me as if I am grossly overweight. What will all my ancestors think? They will consider me some sort of fat pig, and yet in my youth I was the greatest all-round athlete in the whole of England*, if

*A chronicler of the time recorded: 'This colossus of a king draws the bow with greater strength than any man in England, jousts marvellously... is quite exceptional at tennis... hunts with such enthusiasm that he wears out seven or eight horses in a single day's hunt... and he has an extremely strong thigh and calf.'

not the world. Here, let me showeth thee proof.' He thrust the back of his right leg close to Nell's heaving bosom.

'Feel my calf, Nell,' he said. 'Tell me, if it is not still the finest calf thou hath ever felt? Hast thou ever felt such a large swelling?''

Nell gently squeezed the calf through the pink silk hose, and felt that underneath the layers of fat there was indeed quite an impressive muscle.

'Holbein landed me right in the shiteth with one of my wives,' he said. 'His portrait of her made her looketh quite stunningly beautiful, and I agreed to become betrothed to her on the evidence of his painting''. When she arrived from Germany for the wedding she looked like the back of a horse. A very ugly horse. But it was too late to pulleth out, and I had to go through with the ceremony or face being sued for breach of promise. She was so ugly that I did everybody a favour by having her head cut off.'

Nell involuntarily felt her neck, and gulped. She realised she had to handle this suitor with greater care than previous lechers trying to get their hands on her goods. Her usual method of getting rid of them was to knee them in the codpiece, but with king Chopper she

---

'Henry VIII once showed his muscular calf to the Venetian ambassador and asked for his assurance that 'King Francis of France cannot exhibit anything so handsome and swelling.' That would sound too far fetched even for a *Carry On* film.

''Henry selected Anne of Cleves from a portrait painted by Hans Holbein. On seeing her he described her as looking like a 'Flanders mare'. After the wedding night, he recorded: 'I am struck to the heart by her ugliness. I have left her as good a maid as I found her.' The marriage lasted six months.

knew that would be literally risking her neck. There was only one man she was saving herself for, and his name would be kept a secret in her heart until he was free to unlock it. 'What wilt thou do, sire, if thy council refuse to treble thy income?' asked Nell.

'Simple,' said Henry. 'I shall have their heads cutteth off, and then appoint new councillors who wilt grant my request.'

'Thou art very quick to get thy chopper out,' said Nell. 'They do say that thou hath done more chopping than Cardinal Wolsey's father, and he was a butcher.'

'Yea, I intend to chop until I drop,' said Henry, taking Nell's two hands and kissing each of them on the back. 'Well, Nell, I must reluctantly taketh my leave. But I shall return on the morrow to continue my quest to get thee to lie on thy back and think of England.'

'But I never lie on my back or front,' Nell repeated, not adding that she had done it on her knees a few times, usually in the confessional.

Henry felt strangely exhilarated as he strode towards the door. This was the only time he had not done it on the first date, and he found that it hardened rather than weakened his desire to make Nell his gel. 'Until the morrow, fair wench,' he said, blowing a kiss from the door. 'And, Landlord, I suggest that this barrel here needs corking. It hath much movement.'

Claude the Fraud – or Maude the Fraud to his closest or closet friends – looked forward to being corked. Then he would make a full report to Queen Marie. It was the king's cork that was about to be blown.

Henry walked out to the courtyard, jumped for his

horse and missed. This was his sixth fall in as many weeks, and some of his advisors were starting to think that perhaps the bangs on his head were beginning to take their toll*. Their fears would have seemed well founded had they seen this latest fall. He did not even have a horse with him.

Thomas Cromwell and Cardinal Wolsey took King Henry to one side before the meeting with the privy councillors. Cromwell, the Lord Chancellor and the man with his fingers on (and in) the nation's purse, had a deep frown across his face that looked as if it had been ploughed. 'We're d-o-o-m-e-d,' he groaned to the king. 'D-o-o-m-e-d, I tell thee.'

'What on earth's the matter, Cromwell?' said the king, used to him over-reacting to every little crisis. Just the previous month he had almost had a fit simply because Henry had ordered the chopping off of the head of an opponent who had become the first man ever to beat him on the Royal tennis court. 'I did not mind Cardinal Andragassi beating me,' said the king, 'but he laughed when I fell and got my racquet stuck up my baseline.' Cromwell whittered on about the Cardinal being the Pope's personal messenger, but so what? He no longer recognised the Pope and had founded his own Church of England. Now *he* was the closest of all to God, and the Pope did not like it. God, after all, was undoubtedly an Englishman. His independence had got up the Pope's

---

*King Henry had two serious accidents, once when forgetting to close his visor when jousting and the second while out hawking. Modern doctors making a study of his medical notes drew the conclusion that he must have almost certainly suffered brain damage that went untreated.

nostrils, and that was why he had chosen the best tennis player in all of Italy to send to play with him.

'Out with it, Cromwell,' said the king. 'What's gotteth your codpiece in a twist this time?'

'Thou tellest him,' said Cromwell to the hand-wringing Wolsey, who was still sulking over the king taking Hampton Court off him when he had only jokingly offered it as a gift.

'It is indeed bad news, sire,' said Wolsey, whose face was as sombre as a windswept grave. 'The queen hath found out about your latest dalliance, and is demanding a ten thousand crowns payment or she will bloweth all to the *Panorama Times*.'

'And,' added Cromwell, 'she will tell her cousin, King Francis of France, who is just looking for an excuse to come over with his army and give us a good lambasting.'

'Bah!' exclaimed Henry. 'We will sliceth up that frog army with the ease of a hot sword going through camembert.'

Cromwell shook his head sadly. 'But, sire,' he said, 'thou seemeth to have forgotten that we disbanded most of thy army to pay for the building of Hampton Court and to settle Queen Marie's shopping bills.'

'That damned woman,' said Henry. 'How on earth did she findeth out about my latest little adventure? I hardly touched the wench. In fact our only real contact was when she squeezed my muscular calf.'

'That,' said Wolsey, 'is not how we understandeth it. According to reports that the BBC are investigating even as we speaketh, thy Majesty did do unspeakable things with your royal chopper to a lady in waiting called

Baroness Isadora Rubble-Crumpitt.'

'Oh *that* dalliance,' said Henry, relieved that his romance with Nell had not been nipped in the bud. 'That's not worth ten thousand crowns, or even ten thousand groats. She was a lady in waiting in my bed. I only did my royal duty. She was lying there waiting for it and so I giveth her one.'

'One what?' asked Wolsey, perhaps a little naively.

'Why, a royal pardon of course,' said Henry, thinking to himself that if Wolsey believed that he would believe anything.

He believed it. 'In that case I think it appropriate to offer Queen Marie a one thousand crowns payment for the pain she hath suffered,' said the cardinal.

'Her pain?' said Henry. 'What about *my* pain? She hath barred me from the royal bedroom just because I objected to her eating garlic there. She and that sister-in-law are fleecing me of all my money that has been hard-earned by the citizens of this great nation of ours. Their taxes are surely meant for the king, not for a queen who can hardly speak their language.'

'One day a king will cometh to the throne who cannot speaketh or understandeth a single word of English.'

Henry, Wolsey and Cromwell turned as one to look at the speaker, sitting in a corner of this ante-room to the council chamber. It was Bernardo, the king's personal adviser and soothsayer, who was considered by Henry to be a man of great wit and wisdom. In truth he was a charlatan and a complete nincompoop. He held in his hand a crystal glass eye into which he looked with his one good eye to see the future.

'Surely that cannot be true, Bernardo,' said Henry. 'A King of England who cannot speaketh English. What is he then, Scottish? Look again into your eye and see if thou hath made an error.'

Bernardo peered into the eye, and studied hard. 'He speaketh only in the German tongue,' he reported. 'He is named Old King Kohl.'*

'Thou hath astonished and rattled me to my very core,' said Henry. 'Next you will be telling me that the Germans wilt rule Europe.'

'They wilt have a jolly good try,' said Bernardo, looking into his eye. 'But their armies are conquered by a general called Adolf Churchill. It is not until the year of Our Lord nineteen hundred and ninety-seven that the Germans at last taketh full control and form a European Empire in which German is the first language, and there is one currency: the Deutschgroat.'

Henry shook his head in disbelief. 'Enough of the far-off future,' he said. 'What of the morrow? Am I going to get lucky with a wench with a pair that shaketh like jelly? She hath a lovely belly and her name is Nelly. Or perhaps Nell might ringeth a bell.'

Bernardo grimaced as he was dazzled by reflected light from the eye. This was a bad omen. 'I am sorry to have to report, my liege, that Queen Marie will be on the warpath on the morrow,' he said. 'I espyed her talking to a chronicler from the *Panorama Times* and she sayeth things that are so hot that it hath caused a temporary shut down of the powers of my eye. A message came up that

*George I of Hanover could not speak English. He was brought to the throne by an Act of Parliament in 1714 at the age of fifty-five after the fifty other candidates had been ignored to ensure a Protestant succession.

20

sayeth, "Eye, eye that's thy lot."'

'What am I going to doeth?' asked Henry, in such a panic that he was chewing the sleeve of his gold-cloth doublet. 'How can I riddeth myself of this woman? I said months ago we should hath chopped off her head. But no, thou all talketh me out of it just because her Froggie cousin hath a mighty army. Now she setteth out to destroy me in the eyes of my public, the people who loveth and adoreth me and look up to me as a God.'

'Thou must fight like with like,' advised Bernardo. 'Thou art losing out to the Queen in the vital field of public relations.'

'But how do I doeth likewise?' said the king, happy to have somebody else doing the thinking for him. The only time he acted for himself was on the sportsfield or in the bedroom.

'What thou needeth,' said Bernardo, 'is a biographer to record for history as well as for thy subjects what a wonderful and noble man thou art. I will introduce you to a writer friend. We knoweth him as Will the Quill.'

Claude de Bedsop made a note of the name as he crouched under the window disguised as a flower pot.

The privy council studied the parlous state of the royal accounts and decided that King Henry's income should be halved. He then ordered 'off with their heads', but rescinded the order when they agreed to his request for a trebling of his annual allowances.

As the councillors bowed and scraped their way out of the meeting, Hans Holbein captured King Henry on canvas. He was sticking out his tongue.

Will the Winker
A portrait by
Hans Holbein

Toby, or not Toby? That is the question.

What is in a name when a rose smells just

as sweet whatever thou calleth it?

Henry or not Henry?

Marie, or not Marie?

That is the question we must address

Before the morrow brings new arrows

of outrageous fortune.

To write a book, or a play,

Or to take the money and run?

Ay, there's the rub.

22

2

WILL the Quill sat breathless in his favourite writing chair in what served as a study, living room, kitchen, bedroom and garret. From this tiny, cramped rented dwelling in the loft of a rectory alongside St Paul's, the Parish church of Tower Hamlets, he was able to look out on the sweep of the Thames as it flowed on its murky course towards the Tower of London and the Houses of Parliament. Will was out of breath after chasing a goose around the back yard to snatch a quill ready to start scratching the latest chapter in his *The Compleat Historiae of Olde England*.

He had reached the period in which King Alfred burned the rakes. This followed on from Canute failing to hold back the wives, and the adventures of King Arthur and his Naughty Nights before his number was up on the Camelot lottery of life. In a bid to spice it up, he had introduced a torrid love scene between Lancelot and Guinevere in a chapter headed 'Comealot'.

He was convinced there was a market for semi-pornographic history books which would lift them out of their boring rut and bring the past to life. There was a school of thought that his work was more hysterical than historical, but his critics did not understand that he was starting an 'impressionist' movement, giving a view of history as he saw it.

'Facts,' he passionately preached, 'are there as a prop but shouldst never be allowed to getteth in the way of a goodly story.' As with so many of his notions, he was struggling to find anybody who shared his foresight, or even his hindsight.

The hungry writer, who lived on communion bread and wine left over from services at the church next door, had yet to find a publisher for his book, which was a third of the way finished and, so far, stretched to a trifling fifteen thousand, six hundred and three pages. But he was confident that it would be snapped up when it was realised that this was the most graphic chronicle of English history since old Chaucer, the word sorcerer, had penned his *Canterbury Tales*.

Will would have finished his history book by now if it were not for the fact that his mind was always so full of ideas that he could only give twenty-one hours a day to writing. As well as being a prolific wordsmith, he was also an inventor with great vision. In fact he was a man so ahead of his time that there was nobody who could understand his creations.

His latest idea had just been rejected by the dumbheads of Westminster, who were too tied to old, tired traditions. He had suggested introducing what would have been the first postal service in the world. His proposal was that anybody wishing to communicate by letter to a person anywhere in the land could take it to a post office where they would pay a groat for it to be stamped on under a specially engraved heel.

The engraving would be of the king's head, and this would be known as a royal stamp. It would then be delivered by men of letters, but when he pointed out that all doors would have to be fitted with letter boxes it was decided the exercise was too outlandish.

'Pray,' said the thick-skulled man at the patents office, 'wouldst thou want to tell the king that his head is to be stamped on every letter? Next, thou wilt be wanting to licketh his backside.'

Will stamped his heel and walked out of the office in high dudgeon, his right eye twitching furiously. This was how he involuntarily reacted to any anxiety or aggravation in his less than well-ordered life, and the unfortunate habit had earned him the unkind sobriquet of Will the Winker. It had also brought him challenges to duels from husbands thinking he was making advances to their wives, slaps around the face from women taking exception to his presumed effrontery, and the occasional returned wink as an invitation that he was not interested in accepting.

One of the few people Will found to be in accord with him was Bernardo, a soothsayer who had the hairy ear of the King of England. He was due any time now to discuss what he described as a most urgent and top secret assignment. Bernardo had mentioned a possible fee of a golden crown, which was more than he had earned in his entire full-time writing career that he had started after leaving his Stratford, East London home nine years earlier.

He had escaped a loveless marriage into which he had been trapped when he was fourteen years old. A girl next door, Mary Shufflebottom, had invited him to play a game of 'mums and dads'. This involved a make-believe, so he thought, wedding ceremony. How was he to know that the little boy dressed up as a priest was in reality a dwarf who had been ordained in a low church. The oath he took was ruled binding in the eyes of the Roman Catholic church, and he had stuck it for ten years before walking out after his wife had complained that she was still 'the virgin Mary'.

King Henry's decision to start his own church so that he could get a divorce seemed eminently sensible to Will, one of the few wise judgments he had made since inheriting the throne in 1509. He had become an enthusiastic member of the new Church of England in the hope that he would be allowed his freedom. The premature balding, bearded writer had lost his heart to another, but could not give himself completely until he had escaped his marriage.

Will was just about to put quill to parchment to start chapter seven hundred and ninety-eight of his book when Bernardo made what was, to say the least, a strange entrance. He appeared outside the garret window, having taken two hours to clamber up the ivy-clad wall.

Getting over the initial shock of seeing his friend's one-eyed face suddenly appearing above him, Will removed the sackcloth from the window hole and beckoned Bernardo to enter.

It was twenty minutes before he at last made his entry because the window – or rather the hole that was meant to be filled by a window – had not been created to allow entrance to twenty stone of human fat. A window frame it would have accepted with ease, but not such a huge human frame.

'Why hath thou not used the convenience of the

stairs?' asked Will as Bernardo at last dropped in, making the entire rectory shudder to such an extent that a curate downstairs spread panic by shouting that there was an earthquake.

'There are spies around,' whispered Bernardo. 'Things are afoot at the palace, and we must watcheth what we sayeth.'

'Well it would hath to be an exceptionally tall spy to heareth what we have to sayeth up here,' said Will, winking in excitement over what was obviously a momentous issue.

Behind the sackcloth, replaced at the window, Claude de Bedsop listened intently. He was disguised as a chimney pot.

'I am here at the behest of His Royal Highness King Henry,' said Bernardo, bowing in deference. His head was lowered and so he did not see Will make a contemptuous two-fingered gesture. Henry VIII was not his favourite personage. In fact he hated his garters. It was the king who had ordered his father to be beheaded just because he had joined in a little plot to try to blow him to kingdom come. He had vowed that one day he would get his revenge.

'His great and glorious Majesty seeketh a biographer,' explained Bernardo, 'and I hath recommended you as the ideal scribe to paint a word picture of his wondrous deeds, his charitable, unselfish nature, his modesty and benevolence, his philanthropy, his kindness to children and old people, and his sainted life.'

'Uh, whose biography doth thou wanteth me to write?' asked Will.

'Why, King Henry's of course,' said Bernardo.

'Ah,' said Will, his wink going at the speed of a darting bird's wing. 'I did not quite recognise him from the description thou gavest. I would needeth to stretch my imagination as never before. 'Tis not a word picture thou art asking me to paint. 'Tis a tissue of porky pies.'

'No, no, no, no,' said Bernardo, shaking his head so hard that his crystal eye fell out. 'We wilt wanteth thou to tell it warts 'n' all.'

'No restrictions whatever?' said Will. 'I can telleth it as it is about King Chopper?'

'Yea, to a goodeth degree,' said Bernardo. 'Of course, thou wouldst not refer to any of the twelve thousand executions since he cometh to the throne. But thou wouldst be allowed to mentioneth that he hath been ten times voted Man of the Year by the Guild of Executioners, and hath three times won their golden axe outright.'

'What about the way he hath put up the taxes to financeth his opulent lifestyle?' asked Will, causing Bernardo to wince. With the one-eyed Bernardo wincing, and the tense Will the Quill winking they did not make a pretty picture.

'Watcheth thou my lips,' said Bernardo. 'No mention of taxes. Thou wilt be able to write about the way the king taxeths himself in sport and at the hunt, where he hath no peer. Also about his gargantuan appetite. Why, he can out-gorge any man or woman in the kingdom.'

'Can I maketh any reference to his adventures with the ladies?' Will asked, aware of the serialisation value of the king's many conquests.

'Thou canst point out that he is the most handsome monarch in England's long and glorious history,' said Bernardo. 'But thou wilt maketh no allusion to any of His Majesty's fifteen hundred extra-marital liaisons.'

'What about his six marriages?' asked Will.

Bernardo shook his head. 'Refer to him as a gay bachelor,' he said, 'who wilt one day pluck an English rose to dutifully sire an heir to the throne.'

'He hath plucked a fair few already,' said Will. 'No mention even of Queen Marie?'

Bernardo shook his head so hard this time that he almost lost even his good eye. 'Jest thou not,' he said. 'As far as the biography is concerned, she hath never existed. She hath become a pimple on the king's back, and he wisheth to scratch it away.'

'But I thought they hath a marriage madeth in heaven.'

'Hell more like,' said Bernardo. 'Thou must not believe what thou readeth and heareth. The queen putteth about a lot of tales to suit her own purposes. She is interested only in hanging on to the king's purse strings, and she clingeth on to him like a leech to a bleeding limb. Now she planneth to humiliate our great ruler by giving an interview to that radical rag the *Panorama Times*.'

Will gulped. He secretly wrote a column in the *Times* under the pseudonym of the Royal Watcher, which supported calls for England to become a republic. It paid six groats per monthly column, which was Will's sole income. His identity was protected by the editor, Sir Charles Dickhead, because Henry was thirsting for the Royal Watcher's neck. In fact the king had offered a reward of five hundred crowns to anybody who could bring him the Royal Watcher's head on a platter. It was such a tempting reward that Will had wondered about cutting off his own head and taking it to the king, but then he realised what a ridiculous idea that was. How would he see where to put the reward money?

'Well, what sayeth thou?' said Bernardo. 'Wilt thou accept the honour of becoming the king's biographer?'

'I feel in all conscience that I can hath no part of this charade,' said Will. ''Tis beneath contempt that thou should asketh me to paint such a false picture of a man who hath removed more innocent heads than a hundred swords at Agincourt.'

'The fee is *two* gold crowns,' said Bernardo, 'plus a gooseful of quills, and all the ale that thou can sup.'

'When mayst I start?' said Will. Like any man, he had his price.

'Comest thou to Hampton Court Palace on the morrow,' said Bernardo. 'Preparest thou for a long stay. Thou hath much writing to do.'

'What wilt the biography be called?'

'I was hoping thou mayst cometh up with a title,' said Bernardo.

Will thought for a few seconds. 'How about King Chopper?' he said.

'Thou jesteth, of course.'

'Of course. My suggestion would be Henry VIII, Long May He Pisseth Down.'

'Pisseth down?' said Bernardo, his empty eye socket squinting in puzzlement.

'It translates as Long May He Raineth,' explained

Will. 'It is a playeth on words.'

'Not bad,' said Bernardo, 'but it lacketh a little sparkle. We needeth to give Henry an uplifting tag, like Alfred was known as Alfred the Great, and there was Richard the Lionheart.'

Will thought of the most apt title, Henry the Tosser. But he kept this to himself. 'How about Henry, King of Kings and Rogerer of Rogerers,' he said, the words nearly choking him.

'His Majesty wilt be mightily pleased with that,' said Bernardo, 'but omitting the King of Kings line. 'Tis a wee bit twee. Henry, Rogerer of Rogerers it is.'

Bernardo threw his eye in the air in celebration at finding a title. He was frowning when he caught it.

'Dost thou have anybody dwelling on the roof?' he asked in a hoarse whisper.

'Only a coo of pigeons and the occasional moggy,' said Will.

'I just saweth the chimney move, unless my eye deceiveth me' said Bernardo. 'Couldst there be an eavesdropper up there?'

Above them Claude the Fraud cooed and miaowed for all he was worth. A passing pigeon responded by depositing his load on him, and flew off to tell his mates that there was a large bird taking board on the bard's tiles.

Will shrugged. 'What sort of idiot wouldst risketh his neck climbing the ivy to get to my roof?' he said.

''Tis true,' said Bernardo. 'It must hath been a trick of the light.' Idiots did not come bigger than he.

'Hast I shown thee my latest invention?' said Will, reaching beneath the apple box that acted as desk,

31

dining table, couch, workbench and bed. He produced a wooden box on which was pinned a tin plate.

'What is this?' asked Bernardo, studying it with his good eye, while his left eye still looked nervously towards the roof.

''Tis a spinning disc,' said Will, rotating the plate manually.

'What doth it do?'

'It plays records,' said Will.

'Records?' said Bernardo. 'Thou meanst like an accountant's records of the king's debts?'

'Nay, 'tis a musical turntable. Watcheth thou.'

Will leaned close to the plate and sang so that his voice bounced off the spinning plate and resounded around the room. 'Alack, my love thou doest me wrong,' he sang to the tune of 'Greensleeves', 'to casteth me off so discourteously... for I hath loveth thee so long, delighting in thy com-pa-ny.'

'Most impressive,' said Bernardo, his good eye twinkling and his false eye rolling around in his hand in time to the music. 'But why doth thou call it a record?'

'Because I record each song that I singeth in a chart that I am writing,' said Will. 'I will one day have the chart published when I hath recorded my top ten songs.'

'*Your* songs?' said Bernardo, his false eye clouding over. 'But "Greensleeves" is the work of His Majesty King Henry.'' He bowed in deference. Will put up two fingers.

'King Henry was acknowledged as an excellent musician, composer and singer. He was proficient on the lute, harpsichord, spinet and virginals (a form of spinet). It is generally claimed that he composed 'Greensleeves'.

'So he boasteth,' said Will, 'but I penned "Greensleeves" ten years before the king laid claim to it. I named the song after a boy in our hamlet who always wipeth his nose on his sleeve.'

'An important passage of the book wilt be the king's passion for music,' said Bernardo. 'He playeth the lute and harpsichord beautifully.'

'And I hath heard he is a veritable virtuoso on the virginals,' said Will.

Bernardo stood up to take his leave. 'Before thou goeth,' said Will, 'wilt thou cast thy eye on my future as a writer. What wilt be my standing in history?'

Bernardo looked hard into his crystal eye. 'I see Will the Quill acclaimed as the greatest writer ever to put quill to parchment,' said Bernardo. 'That is the good tidings.'

'And the bad tidings?' said Will, still glowing as he thought of his place in history.

'This Will the Quill,' said Bernardo, 'has yet to be born.'*

It was a sulking Will the Quill who showed Bernardo through the sackcloth that served as a door to his garret, and watched him tumble down the stairs. He had forgotten to put his all-seeing glass eye back in.

Bernardo picked himself up, rubbed himself off and hummed 'Greensleeves' to himself as he returned merrily to Hampton Court. He was delighted with the success of his mission, and would report to the king that he had found His Majesty a biographer who would present him

*William Shakespeare was born in 1564, seventeen years after the death of Henry VIII. Several of his finest plays were written during the reign of James I, yet he is popularly known as a giant of the Elizabethan age.

in the best possible light. No warts whatsoever.

He rubbed his hands and eyes together as he reflected on the profit he would make from the project. The king had said that he would pay ten golden crowns as an advance against royalties. The feckless fool had accepted two crowns, which left him with eight crowns for himself. A fat profit for the fat prophet. Why should the writer get all the gold as well as the glory of having his name printed in the tiniest type in the acknowledgements section? Little did Bernardo know, but he was setting the pattern for the procession of publishing agents who would follow in his path.

It was the latest success in a series of mercenary deals by Bernardo, whose life had been transformed on reading a book called *How to Make Enemies and Influence People.* It had been written by Italian statesman Niccolo Machiavelli, and was a guide to taking a short-cut to power and domination. The main thrust of the book was the sound advice that you should trample on anybody who stood in your way in life.

Bernardo had been a humble gardener, known as Bernard the Turnip, at Hampton Court when he first read the book. Taking Machiavelli's advice to extremes, he murdered each of the gardeners who stood between him and the top job until he was promoted to the plum role of the king's Number One fruit and vegetable gardener. The king often visited his orchard for some humpty-rumpty with the kitchen maids, and Henry was impressed at the way the faithful gardener turned a blind eye to his flirtations. Bernard just hoped that the king would not dig too deep with the maids and find where he had buried five murdered gardeners.

He noticed the way foreigners were welcomed to the king's court, such as the German painter Hans Holbein, the Dutch philosopher Erasmus and the Venetian scholar Marco Raphael, and he put an 'o' on the end of his name to give himself a continental image. Then he put it about that he had lost his eye in a jousting tournament, while in actual fact he had knocked it out himself when treading on a garden rake.

King Henry was mad keen on jousting, and on hearing of Bernardo's bad luck invited him to dine with him and share jousting tales. By then Bernardo had chipped a piece of glass off a gypsy's crystal ball and placed it in his empty eye socket. Ever since he had convinced everybody, including himself, that he had a gift for telling the future. He once told the king when looking into his glass eye that he would meet a woman of his dreams the next day (everybody knew that Henry met a woman of his dreams *every* day), and when indeed this did occur His Majesty insisted on Bernardo taking a permanent place at his right hand.

Henry never made a move without first consulting Bernardo, who would look into his glass eye and advise what the morrow had in store. He had quickly learned that the art was to tell the king exactly what he wanted to hear.

Along with Wolsey and Cromwell, he was the most influential man in the king's entourage but he feared his power was going to be undermined by a queen who was questioning the sense of Henry listening so intently to a man who took a one-eyed look at life. Bernardo did not have to look into his glass eye to see that Queen Marie had to go. There was room in the orchard for her.

Will the Quill had just started penning his latest chapter on King Alfred ('Alf was to cooking what Nero was to fiddling... all around him burned...') when he was startled by more movement at his garret window. He looked up to see a French face looking back at him. He knew the nationality because it had become a French window.

'*Bonjour*,' Claude the Fraud said. 'May I drop in to see thee, *mon ami*?'

'There was no need to come through the tradesmen's entrance,' said Will, as Claude lowered himself down from the roof. His silk cloak, breeches and satin doublet were covered in pigeon droppings.

'*Merde*,' he said, explaining his appearance. 'Ze London pigeons are grande sheets, no?'

Will nodded his head. 'They hast certainly done a grand job on thee,' he said.

Claude removed his wide-brimmed hat and bowed low. 'Permit me to introduce myself,' he said. 'Claude de Bedsop, personal equerry to Her Gracious Majesty Queen Marie of England and heir, apparently, to ze French throne.'

'And what mayst I do for thee?' asked Will.

'Her gracious Majesty wishes to give an exclusive interview to ze esteemed *Panorama Times*,' said Claude, an educated man of French letters. 'She wanteth to talk freely and from ze 'eart about 'er sham of a marriage to King 'Enri le Huitième. It is time le grande public Anglais knoweth exactly what kind of a rotten king zey

36

have ruling zem.'

"Tis true,' said Will. 'But how canst I helpeth?'

'As ze famous Royal Watcher, thou art ze ideal man to tell 'er story,' said Claude.

Will was aghast, flabbergasted, befoggled and beflummoxed. 'But how doth thou knowest that?' he said. "Tis a secret betwixt the editor, Charles Dickhead, and myself.'

Claude tapped the side of his nose with a long, slender forefinger. 'Ah, ze little bird telleth me,' he said. 'Ze birds not only shitteth on me, but zey talketh as well. I know zat thou wanteth to expose the king for ze hypocrite and ze squanderer zat he is. Now is thy chance, *mon ami*, through ze luscious lips of Queen Marie.'

Mindful of the book deal that he had just agreed, Will backed off. 'I am sore sorry, but in all conscience I canst be seen to be party to what wouldst be considered in some circles an act of treason.'

'Her Majesty has ordered me to offer a fee of *cinq* golden crowns,' said Claude, more than happy with the five crowns profit that he would make on the deal.

'When mayst I conduct the interview?' asked Will, wondering if perhaps Bernardo had got his services too cheaply.

'Comest thou to Hampton Court Palace on ze morrow,' said Claude. 'Preparest thou for a long stay. Thou hath much writing to do.'

'The king and queen try to decimate each other,' thought Will, 'and I am the pawn in the middle.'

His right eye blinked so much that it very nearly invented moving pictures.

**Will the Winker
A portrait by
Hans Holbein**

Once more on to the beach, dear friends,

As I prepare for a splinter of discontent,

For parting is such sweet sorry.

If you have tears, prepare to shed them

As I walk betwixt and between a King

and a Queen

Who have chosen me to expose their

shallows and miseries.

This is the most unkindest cut of all,

That I am the one left to staunch the

wounds of a marriage made in hell.

3

QUEEN Marie sat in the west wing of Hampton
Court painting her fingernails, which took her
longer than most because she had been blessed with
seven fingers on each hand.* She also had seven toes on
each foot, and while she was not particularly literate
she was exceedingly numerate and could count to
twenty-eight faster than any of her ladies in waiting. She
was also an exceptional harpsichordist, and her seven
finger exercises were the finest ever heard. It was
claimed that she could play the scale of C Major faster
than the ear could hear it, but as nobody had ever heard
it this was difficult to authenticate for the *Book of
Genius Records*.

But for all her talent in doing additions and her
dazzling digital dexterity on the keyboard, Marie was
drowning in a sea of misery and boredom; misery
because she had lost the affection of her husband, and
boredom because all her lovers were away trying to
rekindle the One Hundred Years' War. Why, she
wondered, could they not have sensible six-day wars as
she had heard of in the Middle East?

She had not wanted to enter into the marriage with
'Enri. The union had been forced by her 'andsome,
'unky cousin Francis, King of France, who wanted to
add England to his empire. 'Get 'old of ze daft
Englishman in ze bed,' he had said, 'and give him plenty

*Anne Boleyn, Henry's second wife, had a rudimentary sixth finger
on her left hand – a sure sign, her enemies claimed, that she was an
evil sorceress.

of ze French kisses and ze old hee-haw-hee-haw. You know what zey say, "Get an Englishman by ze balls and his brain will follow." Once you have exhausted him, I will attack with my armies and, *voilà*, England will be mine.'

Why Bon King Francis was so keen to get England she would never know. She had been told that it was a green and pleasant land, but she found it murky and unpleasant. To show off how embracing English air could be, 'Enri had taken her down to Eastbourne on ze South Coast. It was quite quaint, she thought, but not nearly up to ze standard of Cannes, and ze wezzer! It rained throughout zeir two weeks 'oliday in ze royal tent.

It was taking Marie a long time to grow accustomed to ze strange habits of ze English. Ze people surrounding her in court wanted to bathe all ze time and camouflage zeir natural body odours, and zere was not one among zem who had zat wonderfully stimulating garlicy smell that made her ache for France. And zeir food! Ze English were to gastronomy what Christopher Columbus was to clog dancing. Zey were all at sea in ze kitchen, drowning zeir food in gravy so thick that thou couldst cut it with a knife, and cremating zeir meat until all ze goodness had been burned out of it. Zey prepared zeir food like zey made love, in a wham-bang-thank-you-madame style that ruined ze taste and ze flavour. In fact, zey could not cook to save zeir lives, and Marie was convinced that if she had one more morsel of roast beef she would go quite mad.

Zere were two things that made life tolerable for her

on ze throne of England: her freedom to dip into 'Enri's bottomless purse as she wished, and ze love and devotion of ze ordinary people. Why, whenever she went out and about zey would all curtsy to her and wave zeir lace handkerchiefs. Ze women also greeted her warmly.

Marie had wanted to follow her cousin's command to exhaust 'Enri in bed, and was sure she would have found it a great pleasure. He was an exceedingly wide and powerfully built man, attractive not in ze pretty manner of King Francis but in an arousing masculine way. In fact, although Marie was too polite to say it to King 'Enri's face, she considered that he was built like a brick merde-house. She was particularly taken by his fine calves that bulged from his silk hose, and which were only slightly flawed by ze knotted varicose veins that stood out like crooked blue seams.

Despite herself, Marie had lost her 'eart to ze dashing 'Enri, and zey were exceptionally 'appy when zey first wed. Zen, within five minutes of him entering ze marital bed on zeir 'oneymoon night, he had gone as cold as a snowman's nose, and no matter what she tried she could not get him to rise to ze occasion. He had complained that she stank to 'igh 'eaven of garlic, while she was most disappointed to discover that zere was no scent of that great aphrodisiac on his breath. In fact his breath was like that of a sewer rat, but Marie was too much of a lady to make any observation ozer than to gag when he kissed her.

Sitting at a banqueting table with him – a nightly ritual – also made her feel quite ill. He had never been taught table manners, and would think nothing of stuffing an entire pig's head, a sheep's leg and a side of beef down his throat in one sitting during which anybody within a radius of twenty metres was in mortal danger from flying bones. He could do more damage to a rack of boar ribs in five minutes than a bareknuckle fighter in five rounds. Zere was an old French saying *on est ce-qu'on mange*, one is what one eats, and 'Enri was all animal. Next to him, ze royal dogs were ze best fed animals in ze whole of England because at ze end of each meal zere were more bones around ze royal table than in a graveyard. For hours after he had eaten, he would snack on crumbs and chunks of meat that had become trapped in his beard during his two-fisted attack on all that was put before him. Zere had been one terrible occasion when, admittedly befuddled by too many flagons of wine, he had torn apart ze animal in front of him not realising that it was ze 'ampton Court cat. It was ze only time he ever complimented ze chef on ze meal.

Following ze catastrophe of zeir first night togezer, 'Enri had turned to ze table more than to Marie and was much more interested in stuffing himself razer than ze Queen.

Distraught, she had sought advice from her sister-in-law Princess Flirty Of Flanders, who was married to 'Enri's younger brozer Porky, so called because of his chubby face and because he was always telling untruths. Oh yes, and he also liked poking pigs, with a stick of course. Flirty was much more worldy than Marie, and – in ze language of ze day – 'putteth it about a bit'. It was Flirty who had introduced her to ze joys of shopping, and what she called her 'fining' system. 'Any

42

time I findeth Porky telling porkies or having zer bit on zer side – no matter what zer gender, by the way – I fine him by buying myself vunderbar new clozes on his account,' she said in a gutteral accent that sounded as if she had been gargling with steel filings.

Marie followed this rule and in no time at all she had not just a wardrobe full of fine new dresses but whole roomfuls. It was some compensation, but she would much preferred to have been undressing 'Enri razer than dressing herself.

Again she turned to Princess Flirty for ze sort of confidential advice that only a woman of ze world could have given.

'How doth I get ze king to show me 'is ardour?' she asked.

'Harder zan vhat?' said Flirty.

'Not 'arder, but ardour,' said Marie, although 'arder was no doubt what she really meant.

'Hath thou tried wriggling ze most exotic and erotic part of thy body at him?' Flirty asked.

'*Mais oui*, all ze time,' said Marie. 'I shake my *derrière* in his face like a jelly. He say bottoms up, and goeth and 'as a tankard of ale.'

'No, no, not zer backside,' said Flirty. 'I mean hast thou wriggled thy toes at him?'

Marie stopped shaking her *derrière* and shook her head instead.

'Well if he's anyzing like his brozer, he vill love it,' said Flirty. 'Porky is alvays sucking my toes. It driveth us both vild viz desire. And you, viz seven toes, you vill be über der moon.'

43

Flirty raised a warning finger. 'But be very careful,' she said. 'I vas letting zer Palace footman sucketh my toes – after all, vat else iz a footman for? – ven zat 'orrible 'ans 'olbein spotted us and painteth a picture zat appeared in der *Panorama Times*. It got me into gross troubles viz Porky, and he sayeth zat my toes were his by Royal command. I zink zat vill becometh a footnote in history.'

So Marie tried what was known in aristocratic circles as 'ze toe job', but it was an unmitigated disaster. When she stuck ze seven toes of her right foot into 'Enri's mouth he chewed instead of sucking, and she was unable to get one of her size twelve shoes on for a week. It was some time later before Flirty told her that she should have taken her bed socks off first.

Since zen Marie had barred 'Enri from her bedroom. She stuck to ze west wing of Hampton Court, and he to ze east. Her faithful equerry Claude de Bedsop kept a close surveillance on all 'Enri's comings and goings and eavesdropped on his conversations. Marie had ze comfort of knowing her neck was safe because her husband feared ze might of her cousin King Francis. In zis instance, she was relieved that 'Enri was not getting out 'is famous chopper.

She knew that he was plotting to try to divorce her, but she was careful not to give him grounds. Every time she heard that he was dipping his Hampton wick, she demanded a compensation payment from ze Lord Chancellor Thomas Cromwell. He was terrified that she would report ze king's infidelity to her cousin King Francis, who was just looking for an excuse to come over with his vast army and to cut down 'Enri and his cronies. Francis was convinced that ze French could beat ze English in combat, and his personal confidence soared when 'Enri visited Norzern France for a great festival of peace in 1520. Zey 'ad a friendly wrestling match and French observers reported that Francis 'ad got much ze better of ze duel and 'ad thrown 'Enri on to his broad back. English observers were warned that zeir 'eads would be parted from zeir shoulders if zey as much as whispered of zis 'umiliation.*

Marie glanced at ze prototype pendulum clock that took up ze entire far wall of her drawing room. It was nearing midday and zere was no sign of ze essayist that Claude de Bedsop had órganised to visit 'er for an interview that was to be published exclusively in ze *Panorama Times*. She 'ad decided to tell all about zeir marriage in a bid to shame 'Enri into returning to ze marital bed. Crafty Marie knew zat with ze public on 'er side 'Enri would never dare get out his chopper to part her from her *tête*. But it just might stir 'im into doing his duty as an 'usband.

She was ready to reveal all, but where on earth was zis Will ze Quill whom Claude 'ad 'ired at great expense?

While Queen Marie was waiting in the west wing, Will the Quill was a quarter of a mile away in the east wing

*This festival was the historic Field of the Cloth of Gold organised by Cardinal Wolsey to improve the *entente cordiale* between England and France after years of war. King Henry and King Francis did, indeed, have a friendly wrestling match, and Francis did, indeed, throw the King of England. And it was not reported at the time by any England observer for fear of Henry's chopper.

noting down the demands of King Henry. It had been agreed that Will would write the book but that it would appear as the King's own work, with no reference to a ghostwriter. 'If thou as much as whispereth that the book is anything but mine own,' warned Henry, sucking in a chunk of mutton from his beard, 'thou wilt writeth thine own death warrant. Thou wouldst get the treatment that awaiteth that accursed Royal Watcher. When, and it is only a matter of time, the traitor is captured I will personally chop off his head. 'Tis a long time since I enjoyeth a good chopping spree.'

Will winked rapidly and felt quite ruffled as he ran a finger around his ruff. He was only too delighted not to have his name on the book, although he would have liked a share of the Royal royalties that the greedy king had insisted were all to go into his pocket. Henry had decided to make a Royal decree that everybody in the land would have to purchase a copy of the book, so it was fairly certain to go straight to the top of the best sellers list, beating even the sales of Robin Hood's kiss 'n' tell autobiography: *My Gay Nights in Tights with the Knights*. This was a sequel to his first best seller, *How the Merrie Men Made Marian*.

The interview with King Henry had got off to a bad start because of a simple mix-up. The king thought that Will was the new doctor come to check on a personal problem.

'I keep getting a pain in my plums,' said Henry, dropping his breeches and revealing his private parts to a fairly surprised Will. 'Just have a feeleth and telleth me what thou thinketh.'

Will knew better than to ignore a Royal command, and so he squeezed the king's plums.

'Well, what dost thou thinketh?' asked Henry.

'Uh, very nice,' said Will, not quite sure how to respond.

'I *know* they're nice,' said Henry. 'They are the best plums in the whole of England, but do they needeth treatment? Perhaps some ointment?'

Will made a closer inspection, and had them back in his hand just as Bernardo entered the room.

'What on earth art thou doing with the Royal testicles in thy hand?' asked a shocked and jealous Bernardo. He had never been allowed this sort of familiarity.

'What doth it look liketh he is doing?' said the king. 'He is inspecting the Royal plums.'

'But thou cannot alloweth this sort of thing in the book,' said Bernardo. 'It would destroyeth thy public image.'

'I doth not wish him to write about them,' said Henry. 'I just beseech him to maketh them better. Canst thou help me, doctor?'

'Doctor?' chorused Will and Bernardo.

'This is not thy doctor,' said Bernardo. 'This is thy ghostwriter, Will the Quill.'

'Unhand me this instant, sire,' bellowed the king. 'How dare thee lay hands on the Royal plums.'

Will pulled back, bowing and blushing. 'Forgive me, thy Majesty,' he said. 'I did only what thou commandeth.'

It was all they could do to stop King Henry getting his chopper out there and then. He was purple of face as well as plums as he pulled up his breeches, and put his face into Will's face. 'Thou art the first of my male subjects to hold the Royal plums,' he said through teeth caked with chicken, beef, lamb and boar from his last meal. 'If ever thou breatheth a word to a single living being I wilt cut thy plums off and stuff them where the sun doth not shineth.'

There was a little bit of an atmosphere as they got down to discussing the book, but the incident was soon forgotten as the king put all his concentration on talking about his life and times.

Henry chose the title himself: *Henry the Magnificent*, and after four hours they had agreed on the first sentence of the first chapter:

> *I, Henry the Magnificent, King of Kings, Defender of the Faith, mightiest man walking this earth, singer of songs, musician extraordinaire, handsome (but not at all effeminate like Francis of France), the greatest athlete, swordsman, jouster and hunter in all of England, nay of Europe, master of all I survey and exceedingly well hung, was born in extremely humble circumstances.*

It was agreed that Henry needed to be seen to have overcome early obstacles and hardship, and to leave out the bit about him inheriting his father's fortune as well as the throne, along with his dead brother's widow. He wanted to be portrayed as a man of the people who had got where he is today by sheer endeavour. The fact that he had never done a day's work in his life was neither here nor there.

"Tis very important when I am writing this book,' said Henry, 'to depict myself as a man of great vision, which I am of course, and also somebody who canst overcome any problem, cross any river, climb any mountain, clear any obstacle and defeat any foe.'

Will would have been slightly more impressed by these statements had the king not been crawling round the room on his hands and knees as he talked. He punctuated his sentences with barking noises, and just a couple of times Will had to kick out quite sharply to stop him from biting at his ankles. The bottom line was that the king was barking mad.

'What thou art observing,' confided Bernardo when Henry went for a Royal wee (up against a tree in the garden, incidentally), 'is the result of the king suffering a fall too many from his horse. Not a word of this must be repeated to a soul. Canst thou imagine what the Royal Watcher wouldst make of this in his vitriolic anti-Establishment column?'

Will could not only imagine it; he would bring it to reality at the first opportunity.

'How hast thou managed to keep his condition from the public thus far?' he asked.

'He drinketh a potion made up for him by the court medicine man, who betweeneth you and me is even madder than the king,' Bernardo explained. 'It keepeth him sane for days on end, but when the effects weareth off... well, you hath seen for yourself what occureth. There was an occasion recently when we loseth track of him. We found him entered in a greyhound race on Richmond Green. He cameth third out of trap three, and we all lost our money. If only he could have drawn trap one.'

The king was almost rational when he returned from the Royal chamber, having drunk his potion. 'What I suggesteth is that thou goest away and writeth out that first sentence so that I can readeth it in the clear light of morning,' he said to Will. 'I must away. I hath an important appointment.'

Bernardo consulted his glass eye. 'Yea,' he said, nodding his head. 'Thou wilt be meeting a wench who hast stolen thy heart.'

'Thou knoweth everything, Bernardo,' sayeth the king. 'But here is something thou knowest not. If thou mentioneth a word about the wench to Queen Marie thy head wouldst be off in the twinkling of an eye. Doth I maketh myself clear?'

'As clear as crystal,' said Bernardo, staring into his glass eye.

'As for thee,' Henry said, turning to Will the Winker, 'if thou winketh at me once more I wilt have thy neck on the block. Porky may be a little bit that way inclineth, but I hath not an ounce of nancy in me.'

King Henry then slipped on a false black beard, and left the room by a side window. He decided he would walk to the Peacock and Partridge today. This way, he would not fall off his horse.

It was another two hours before Will found his way to Queen Marie's room in the west wing. He had asked an ancient royal gardener the way. 'It be beyond that hedge over yonder,' he said, pointing with a crooked finger that seemed to go in several directions at once. Will went beyond the hedge, and then beyond the next hedge, and then beyond another hedge and then another, and another, and beyond another before he realised that he was hopelessly lost in the Hampton Court maze. 'This,' Will thought, 'is beyond a joke.' Now he understood the phrase 'hedged in'.

He was about to disappear with a flash and a bang up his own breeches when he accidentally stumbled over a footman and a downstairs maid doing amazing things to each other in the maze beyond another hedge. They too were lost: in ecstasy. The footman first of all offered his grateful thanks to Will for treading on him, and then pointed him to the exit without using his hands. Will winked at the footman and at what was clearly a handmaid, and his eye was going like the clappers by the time he had at last extricated himself from a maze that he considered a hedge too far.

King Henry was later to explain that he had grown all the hedges for his hogs, a fact which just amazed Will. It gave him an idea for a future project in which he would write a series of short stories while in the maze. He would call them *Postcards from the Hedge*.

Queen Marie was playing a two-handed solo duet on the harpsichord when he was ushered into her room that was hung with enough drapes to have exhausted an entire colony of silk worms.

'Ah, *bonjour* Monsieur Quill,' she said, waving her seven-fingered right hand while continuing to play the full extent of the keyboard with her left. Her fourteen toes, encased in one of the three thousand pairs of shoes she had bought in the last month, were tapping in time to the music, causing the chandeliers in the ceiling above her head to shake. She had a huge bejewelled ring on each finger, and these gave a percussion accompaniment as she clattered up and down the keyboard at the speed of light.

Will had never seen her in the flesh before, and he was surprised at how Hans Holbein's portraits flattered her. One of the Holbein portraits had portrayed her as so voluptuous that the *Panorama Times* had printed it on their comely page three, but to the naked eye she looked as flat as a Shrovetide pancake. In fact he would not have believed that it was Queen Marie had it not been for the unmistakeable wide, blue staring eyes that were saucer size in a face that seemed to have shrunk since her last portrait had been painted.

Marie walked from the harpsichord and beckoned Will to join her on the chaise longue. Her dress seemed several sizes too large as she sat alongside him, lost in a shower of silk.

'*Alors*, Monsieur Quill,' she said, 'I see by ze look in *votre* eye zat I am not so *grande* as thou expected, non?'

Will averted his gaze because she was starting to return his wink. The waft of garlic coming from her mouth was enough to knock over an army.

'I hath to admit, thy Majesty,' he said, 'that I believeth thou to be a much less, uh, dainty Queen.'

'My appearance is all ze fault of zat 'orrible 'usband of mine,' she said. 'He hath caused me such stress zat I am shedding weight by ze 'our. My doctor 'e zays it is somezing to do wiz bulemia, but I 'as never ever been zer. I wanteth thou to maketh zis clear in ze article zat thou will writeth.'

Will made copious notes as the queen described in detail the problems she was having with Henry, speaking with an accent so heavy that he decided it had to be because every word was weighed down with garlic. She had been taught to speak English by Princess Flirty from Flanders, and her patois was a strange mix of hee-haw French and pig-gutteral German. 'He thinketh more of 'is 'orses zan me,' she said, wiping away the hint of a tear with the sixth finger on her right hand. 'He is always going off on ze 'unts, and is up and down on ze 'orse much more zan on me.'

The queen moved closer to Will, opened her royal-blue eyes wide enough to have let the cat in, and whispered in a confidential tone. 'Zis marriage,' she said, 'it is too crowded.'

'Crowded?' said Will, removing the handkerchief from his nose and then quickly replacing it as a gale of garlic blew his way.

'Oui,' said Marie, 'it is not just 'Enri and me. Zer are ozzers.'

'Ozzers?' said an intrigued Will.

'Oui, at least zirty-zree zat I know of,' she said. 'He is always doing ze naughties wiz zem.'

'And, pray, what exactly are these ozzers?' said Will.

'*Alors, filles*, of course,' the queen revealed.

'Fillies?' said Will, even more amazed than he was in the maze. 'Thou meanest the king doth hath thirty-three fillies and that he doth do IT with all of them?'

The queen nodded sadly, her chandelier-size diamond earrings shaking in time and sympathy with her nodding head.

'Oui,' she said. 'And zer may be many more. He is always, 'ow you English say, dipping the dick.'

Will thought she meant wick, but the Queen knew exactly what she meant.

She moved even closer, so that Will could now feel her bony legs through the layers of silk dress. 'I tell thee somezing else,' she said conspiratorially. 'Ze king is always talking to ze trees, and he often pee-pees up zem as well.'

Will was inclined to believe this after seeing his barking mad performance earlier in the day.

He had almost worn out his quill with his notes, and begged his leave so that he could hurry back to his garret and get the interview and his Royal Watcher column written in time to catch the Caxton press.

'But thou must not goeth already,' said the queen. 'I am flattereth by thy saucy winking, and I zink zer is much more we could discuss on ze royal bed, *non*?'

If she had had a little more flesh on her, Will had to confess to himself that he would have been tempted. Bouncing up and down on a bed with her would have been like a dog playing with a bone. Anyway, his heart belonged to another, and he would save himself for her. He decided, in the best traditions of reporters throughout time, to make his excuses and leave.

'I thanketh thee for the invitation, thy Majesty,' Will said, bowing and kissing her hand and having a devil of a job extricating his beard from her maze of bejewelled fingers. 'I hath much handwriting to do to catch the press.'

Marie did not hide her displeasure. 'I was 'oping thou could showst me exactly how thy quill, Will, works,' she said, giving him a full blast of garlic from two paces. 'Surely thou hast time for ze special massage zat I give. Thou hath never been properly felt until thou hath had my fourteen fingers exploring thy body.'

'Another time perhaps, thy Majesty,' said Will, bowing and backing away towards the door as quickly as he could in reverse. He did not see the surviving Hampton Court cat that Henry had not yet got around to devouring and, as he tripped over it, the moggy emitted a loud wail. Her Majesty's ladies in waiting in the adjoining room looked at each other in a knowing and envious way.

Queen Marie, they thought, had hath her way again.

But Will had his mind on hathing his way with another. And, no, her name was not Hathaway.

**Will the Winker
A portrait by
Hans Holbein**

Would she were fatter, Queen Marie
might be compared to a summer's day.
Nay, but it is winter that hangeth on her
bones, and methinks she has a lean and
hungry look, unlike yon husband of hers
Whose very presence maketh mine hair
stand on end and my neck fair ache.
I will toil at my parchment to bring forth
All that I knowest about the King,
So that the public understandeth
He were born a fool and remaineth thus.

4

THE latest issue of the *Panorama Times* dropped on the desk of Cardinal Wolsey like a barrel of gunpowder. The front page splash was an exclusive interview with Queen Marie under the huge banner headline: HENRY HAS HIS OATS WITH THE HORSES. It was accompanied by a reconstruction drawing by Hans Holbein showing the King sleeping alongside a frisky grey mare, and underneath was the caption, 'A horse, a horse, my kingdom for a horse.'

In the interview, Queen Marie made the astonishing claim that King Henry was 'carrying on' with a string of horses and that she felt crowded out of their marriage. There was even worse inside, where the wretched Royal Watcher had dared suggest in his anti-Royal column that the king had gone barking mad. 'A Hampton Court insider,' he wrote, 'hath told me of strange occurrences at the Palace. The king doth barketh, beggeth for bones and needeth to be taken for walkies. Is this the man we wanteth as king of all England, a man who doth sleepeth with horses, doth barketh like a dog and doth have more chance of siring a foal than a son?'

Wolsey's face turned as purple as his cassock as he read the revelations. He knew that if the king were to be kicked off the throne he would quickly be divested of all his power and the vast riches that went with it. Perhaps even divested of his head. It was vital that the king be kept on the throne, even though Wolsey felt that he personally was much better suited to the job of ruling over the country.

He summoned Lord Chancellor Cromwell, who had already seen a copy of the magazine. ''Tis treasonable,' said Wolsey. 'Quite monstrous.'

'Ooooh, I agree,' said Cromwell. 'Fancieth doing it with gee-gees. What on earth doth his Majesty thinketh he is doing. His subjects will considereth that he hath become unstable.'

'I mean 'tis monstrous this scandal sheet should publish such untruths,' said Wolsey, slamming the magazine down on his desk top. 'Heads wilt rolleth for this.'

'We must maketh sure the king doth not see the articles or it could be our heads,' said Cromwell. 'He expecteth us to protecteth him from this sort of publicity.'

Too late. The door swung open and the king came in on all fours with the magazine clamped between his teeth. 'I wanteth the heads of the people responsible for this,' he said, dropping the *Times* at Wolsey's feet. 'First, off with the queen's head, then off with the kopf of that traitor Hans Holbein. I wanteth him hung and quartered but not drawn. Then I demandeth not just the head but also the dangly bits of the Royal Watcher.'

'Thou canst not take the queen's head, nay, neither even a hair of it,' said Wolsey. 'King Francis would invade us with his French army within hours of her head dropping into the basket. She also hath the sympathy of the public now that they knoweth the secret of thy liaison with the Royal horses.'

'But 'tis gross exaggeration,' said the king, now lying under the desk panting. 'I hath not done it with thirty-three horses. One or two, perhaps, but that French mare is lying through her garlic breath to suggesteth that I hath been involved with so many of my mounts.'

'What we needeth,' said Wolsey, throwing a biscuit under his desk to keep the king happy, 'is somebody who canst infiltrate under cover and informeth us about the *Panorama Times*. We hath been trying for more than a year to findeth out who art behind it, but my spies faileth me. It needeth to be an established writer, who canst pretendeth that he desireth to scribble unkindly about our king.'

'I shalt have his head off,' growled Henry from under the desk.

'No, my liege,' said Wolsey, 'there wilt be no need of that. This shalt be a friend who wilt just purporteth to be thine enemy. As soon as he hath made contact with the perpetrators of this pirate paper we shalt sendeth in the king's guards and have them locked up in the Tower.'

'What about Will the Quill?' said Bernardo, who had been sitting quietly in the corner contemplating his crystal eye.

'Why shouldst he be locked up in the Tower?' asked Cromwell.

'No, I meanst why not employeth him as the spy?'

'A good idea,' said Wolsey. 'We shall suggesteth it to him after his meeting with the king this noon day when they wilt be discussing the second sentence of the book. If we are to combateth the public relations expertise of

59

the queen I think we will need the book to be written just a little quicker. I hath worked it out that at the present rate, it will be ready for the press sixty-seven years from now.'

Bernardo took Henry by a lead to get his sanity-restoring potion, and Wolsey and Cromwell went in search of Hans Holbein, whose graphic drawing had added extra weight to the queen's allegations against the king.

Hans Holbein was never happier than when he had a brush in his hand. Sometimes, to amuse friends, he would paint with the brush between his teeth and make them laugh by saying, 'Look, no hans.' Yes, he was a merry old soul, who always drew a large crowd.

He had joined King Henry's court first as a decorator, but he had since established himself as His Majesty's chief portrait painter with a special commission for capturing any pretty ladies he saw on canvas. He would then show the finished painting to the king and if His Majesty felt drawn, so to speak, to any of the ladies, Hans would arrange a private meeting. So far, there had not been a single lady whom the king had not fancied.

This procurement by portrait had led to the occasional embarrassing episode. Henry had been so taken by one of the paintings that he married the subject of the portrait on the strength of how Hans had portrayed her on canvas. What Hans had never dared divulge was that the lady in question, Anne of Cleves, was not available for a sitting when he went to Flanders to paint her and so, as he had claimed expenses for the trip, he substituted a face and a body from his imagination.

He could not believe how ugly the real Anne was when she arrived in England for her betrothal. The king was even more shocked. She could have haunted for Germany. Hans paid the ladies in waiting a bonus for covering her face in veils, but Henry was not a fool. Well, not a complete fool but he was working on it. He quickly discovered that she was as ugly as sin, and the marriage lasted just six months.

Hans told Henry that he had obviously caught her on a good day. 'A good day?' roared the king. 'A good day? Even at her very best and in the fading light of evening she couldst not hath looked as appealing as a dead pig that had been stuffed and bled dry. In fact, givest thou me the dead pig any day.'

The king growled at a trembling Hans. 'Just considereth thyself lucky that I hath not had thy head chopped off,' grumbled Henry, whose only compensation was that his wife's looks gave him a lot of new material for his after-dinner speeches to his courtiers.

'My wife,' he would say with a court jester's style of delivery, 'is so ugly that the mirror refuseth to reflecteth her image. When she was born I understandeth that the midwife slappeth her mother. She hath calves that only a cow would love, and her teeth are liketh the stars. They cometh out at night. When she goeth to the doctor he looketh in her mouth and doth instructeth her to say, "Moo!" On her wedding day I hath twenty-one guns fired. Sadly they all misseth her. I wanteth to toast her at our wedding reception, but I was adviseth that it was

61

not quite the place for a cremation. She now considereth herself half English and half French, and so she shaveth under only one arm. As for the hair on her top lip, I hath asked her to leave it there so that I hath somewhere to put my bedtime snack. She hath so much hair on her face that I hath somewhere to wipeth my hands without need of a towel. I hath given her a porcupine for her birthday. 'Tis the only pricks she'll be getting from me. She is so ugly that the cat doth putteth her out at night.'

German-born Hans Holbein had moved to London on the recommendation of Sir Thomas More, who had told King Henry that he was the greatest painter of the age. Hans felt somewhat put out when His Majesty had assigned him to the job of painting the walls and ceilings at Hampton Court, and he was still having to do the odd bit of decorating to earn his daily bread.

On the day that the *Times* articles appeared, Hans was painting the ceiling of a bedroom in the west wing of Hampton Court with his bucket of paint jammed on the top of the door. How was he to know that Wolsey and Cromwell were going to burst in like bats out of hell? The door swung open, the bucket toppled and the paint poured on to the cardinal and the Lord Chancellor, turning them both a fetching shade of primrose yellow.

'Ein thousand apologies, your Lordships,' said Hans, coming down his ladder and removing the bucket from the head of Wolsey, who got the worst of the load. It was believed that it was this incident that triggered the saying, 'bucketing down'.

Wolsey's face was red with rage, which, mixed with the yellow paint, gave him an orange glow. 'If 'tis not enough that thou art a traitor,' he roared, 'thou art also a would-be assassin, attacking the two senior servants of His Glorious Majesty Henry VIII of England.'

All three men bowed their heads respectfully.

'I know nicht vat thou talketh about,' said Hans, who had been on Wolsey's hit list ever since he had painted a life-like portrait of him that the podgy, frump-faced cardinal thought made him look podgy and frump-faced. 'Ich bin a loyal subject to zer most vunderbar king in all zer vorld.'

Wolsey produced the now yellow pages of the *Panorama Times*. 'Art thou going to deny that this is thy work?' he said, pointing a yellow finger at the sketch of the king lying asleep alongside the now yellow mare.

'Ja, zat ist alles mein own verk,' said Hans. 'How did it get into zis megazine, and vere do I send mein invoice?'

'When didst thou draw this obscene scene for the yellow press?' asked Cromwell.

'Ein year ago,' said Hans. 'Zer king vanted a drawing of himself vith his favourite horse. Zey hath doctored my drawing, bringing zem much closer togezzer.'

'And how doth thou explain that this scandal sheet hath it?' asked Wolsey.

'Alles ich knoweth ist zat zer king auctioned it after making vun of his gross funny after-dinner speeches,' said Hans. 'He vanted to raise money, he told us, for zer home for fallen vomen zat he set up in London. All zer vomen come under his patronage.'

'Who purchaseth the drawing?' said Cromwell.

Hans shrugged. 'As I remember it, zer buyer was a Frenchman who vas over on ein visit to zer queen,' he said. 'But I knoweth nicht his name.'

Claude de Bedsop, hidden out of sight under the four-poster bed, moved uncomfortably. He hoped that the purchase could not be traced to him. The editor of the *Panorama Times* had paid him a gold crown for the publications rights to the drawing. How was he to know that they would change the drawing so that it looked as if the king and the horse were very close together in the stable.

'Considereth thyself lucky that thou hath a rational defence,' Wolsey said to Holbein, 'otherwise I would hath taken the greatest pleasure in presiding over thy execution. Carry on painting.'

Just at that moment Daisy, the chambermaid, came in. She fell over the bucket on the floor and tumbled into Hans, bringing him to his knees. He said that it had given him an idea for a song: 'Hans, Knees and Boomps-a-Daisy'.

'For that,' said Wolsey, 'thou deserveth to hath thy head cut off.'

Cromwell and the hidden Claude de Fraud nodded in agreement.

The second paragraph of the first chapter of *Henry the Magnificent* took the little matter of six hours to construct. If Will the Quill and the king had been left to get on with it, the time spent on the composition might have been at least halved, but Cardinal Wolsey and Lord Chancellor Cromwell – each with a face as yellow

64

as the parchment on which Will was scratching –
insisted on putting in their two groatsworth.

Will wanted to point out that you could not write a
book by committee, but he did not wish to provoke
unnecessary friction because he already sensed that
there was something of an atmosphere over the little
matter of the articles in the *Panorama Times*.

He had pretended to be shocked to the point of
incredulity when he was shown the articles that he,
privately, considerered the finest he had ever written.
'Let us hurrieth and get the king's book out in response
to this propaganda,' he urged, knowing full well that at
the current rate of progress they would all be dead and
buried long before the first chapter was finished.

After long and at times acrimonious argument, this
was the agreed second paragraph of the first chapter of
the book:

*I was very close to my mother when I was born.
In fact she was in the same bed. My early
childhood was one of bitter struggle, but then, at
the age of seventeen, I – because of my natural
intelligence, strength of character and all the
qualities you would expect in a great leader –
thoroughly earned my place on the throne of
England following the demise of my father, Henry
VII. I was able to comfortably handle my new
responsibilities because of the loyal and unstinting
support and guidance of my two most trusted
servants, Cardinal Wolsey and Thomas Cromwell.
Let me make the point very early on, for the*

65

purposes of historical accuracy, that Cardinal Wolsey, Thomas Cromwell and I are all much better looking and more physically attractive than you would gather from looking at the Hans Holbein portraits of us. In fact, there is not one of my subjects who would dispute my claim to being the most handsome and desirable man in the whole of England.

Will the Quill personally thought that to introduce Wolsey and Cromwell so early into the story was, to say the least, confusing to the reader, but he was outvoted two to one, with the king abstaining because he was too busy eating his lunch out of the dog dish.

Once the paragraph had been edited and polished, Will asked permission to be excused so that he could get it prepared on the special publishing parchment.

'Before thou goeth,' said Wolsey, 'we hath an assignment that the king doth wanteth thee to undertake.'

'What wouldst that be?' asked Will, gathering together his quills and parchment notepaper on which were three hundred crossed-out paragraphs where they had continually changed their minds as to what should be written about the king.

'We wanteth thee to get thyself employment on the *Panorama Times*,' said Wolsey. 'Once thou hath made thy infiltration, givest us the nod and we will moveth in and arresteth everybody in sight. Most of all we wanteth the head of the Royal Watcher.'

Will gulped. 'But how doth I do that?' he asked. 'The

Times is an underground magazine. Nobody knoweth who doth produceth it.'

''Tis quite simple,' said Wolsey. 'Get the BBC – the British Broadcasting Criers – to announce that thou wanteth to write for the magazine. Thou wilt then be certain to be approacheth by a representative, and thou canst tell them that thou wisheth to write some anti-king articles.'

'And I wilt order thy head to be cut off,' said Henry, who was half-dozing under the table.

'Taketh no notice of the king,' said Wolsey. 'All that doth interesteth him is the head of the Royal Watcher.'

'But my hands are too full,' protested Will, desperate to get off the assignment. 'I cannot possibly taketh on such a mission when I have to giveth my full concentration to writing the king's book.'

'I am writing my own book,' growled the king, snapping at Will's ankles. 'All thou hath to do is provideth the words.'

'But...' said Will.

'No buts,' said Wolsey. 'There is the five hundred crowns reward if thou findeth the Royal Watcher, plus another ten crowns as a guaranteed fee.'

'I shall start to looketh on the morrow,' said Will, wondering to himself if perhaps he was getting in just a little too deep. He was ghostwriting the king's book (or, rather, providing the words for it), had interviewed the queen and was responsible for the Royal Watcher's column. Now he had accepted the job of tracking down the Watcher. How, he wondered, should he go about looking for himself?

**Will the Winker
A portrait by
Hans Holbein**

All the world's a stage and I am but a bit
player in life's rich pageant,
Treading the boards warily for fear I
mayst cause offence.
Yet here I find myself thrust into a
leading role for which I hath no appetite.
'Tis my neck that is under the shadow of
Henry's threatening axe,
But I am not yet ready to shuffle off this
mortal coil, and I shall yet surpriseth
with my cunning.

68

5

CHARLES Dickhead had founded the *Panorama Times* in 1525 as a radical voice against the monarchy, and against the lavish excesses of the king and his court. He had started it as a single sheet, printed covertly in his spare time on the Caxton press at the head office of the British Broadcasting Criers organisation where he worked as a 'tidings writer' and as an occasional news crier. It was at the BBC where all the government and royal propaganda was collated, and then circulated on scrolls to town criers throughout the land. 'Hast thou got the scrolls?' would come the shout. 'No, 'tis just the way that I walketh.'*

Dickhead's had at first been a lone voice in the wilderness, but when the king started collecting and rejecting wives as if they were little more than bedsocks the *Times* rapidly grew in popularity. There were many who did not like the way King Henry meddled with the prayer book and twisted the outlook and teachings of the Church to his own selfish needs, but they were frightened to speak out for fear of losing their head.

There were many more who were absolutely appalled by the extravagance of the king and those surrounding him. While thousands lived in hovels, he and his cronies lavished millions of crowns – lifted from the tax treasury and stolen from the dissolved monasteries – on building vast homes and palaces.

*© Morecambe and Wise and their scriptwriter Eddie Braben, circa 1970.

As if the one thousand rooms of Hampton Court were not sufficient for any man's needs, Henry transformed Whitehall Palace into the largest palace in the Western world. At the same time he took over the neighbouring site of the Hospital of St James, and built in its place the far more useful St James's Palace, and then embarked on erecting the Palace of Nonsuch in Surrey, a bizarre turreted pleasure dome with an inner court dominated by a larger-than-life statue of himself. Bernardo had looked into his crystal eye and prophesised that it would become the forerunner of a place called, apparently, Dizzyland.

The *Times* voiced the dissatisfaction of all those who had the conscience and the courage to be opposed to this excessive expenditure, and the circulation gradually grew until it was selling as many as two hundred copies every month. Dickhead had a Caxton press hidden in the basement of his home at Blackfriars, and produced the eight-page magazine while continuing his everyday cover job as a tidings writer and occasional news crier at the BBC.

He had the help of a staff of one, Will the Quill, who worked for him on a freelance basis and wrote the Royal Watcher column which was the most widely read feature in the magazine.

Sadly, there was just one drawback with Charles Dickhead being the leader of the radicals who were in the mood for revolt against the king: he was as mad as a March hare, as crazy as a loon, as silly as a candle with no wick, as daft as a brush, as nutty as a fruitcake. Yea, he was positively potty. This, of course, made him eminently suited to the BBC.

For a man whose main work was shrouded in secrecy, he was exceedingly loud. His training as a town crier had rendered him incapable of saying anything quietly, and he prefaced every statement by shouting, 'Oyez, oyez, oyez. Hear ye...'

He had always tended towards eccentricity, a prerequisite it seemed for working at the BBC, and he finally parted company with sanity one afternoon when announcing the king's fourth marriage from the town hall steps at Greenwich. The news had so annoyed him that he had shaken his bell too hard. The clapper inside the bell had worked itself loose, and came flying out like a stone from a catapult and struck Dickhead straight between the eyes.

'Hell's bells,' he was heard to cry, as he dropped unconscious. He refused medical aid, and after coming to insisted on carrying on with his announcement. There were those in the audience who feared he had done some damage to his brain when he shouted, 'Oyez, oyez, oyez. Hear ye that our randy King Henry VIII hath got his royal leg over yet again. A sumptuous wedding banquet is to be held payeth for out of thy pocket, but wilt a morsel cross thy lips? Wilt a single drop of claret touch thy tongue? Wilt it bollocketh.'

It was at that moment that he was led away from the townhall steps and shuffled off back to the BBC, where it was advised that he should be given less of a high profile role in future. He was demoted from head town crier, a very big noise indeed at the BBC, and concentrated on writing the news – often with a near treasonable slant – and giving outside broadcasts only when no other criers were available. But once a crier, always a crier and the volume of his voice appeared to increase rather than diminish as he grew older and less wise.

Will the Quill had quickly recognised the security dangers involved in having a conversation with Dickhead within one hundred yards of any possible eavesdropper, and would never talk to him on any important issue if there was even the slightest chance of anybody overhearing. It meant that they had some fairly bizarre exchanges, peppered with meaningless comments dropped in to confuse any possible bystander.

Following his appointment by the king to seek out the Royal Watcher, Will arranged to meet Dickhead in the middle of Blackheath Common at noon. He felt that within its one hundred acres there was a reasonable chance that they could find some place where they would not be overheard.

From a distance of some one hundred and fifty yards away, Dickhead spotted Will. 'Oyez, oyez, oyez,' he shouted, making heads turn across the Common. 'Hear ye that I am delighteth to seeth thee old chap. The *Times* selleth like hot cakes this month. All the king's horses could yet bringeth down randy Henry.'

Will, his winking right eye working overtime, put a finger to his lips as Dickhead greeted him with a warm handshake. 'Watcheth thou thy tongue,' said Will. 'The king hath a spy on the looketh out for the Royal Watcher.'

Dickhead looked all around. There was not another

soul in sight. 'Well he's hardly likelieth to heareth us here,' he boomed.

'But he wilt just that, taketh my word for it,' said Will, and then speaking in a whisper. 'For thou seest, sire, I am he.'

'Thou art who?' shouted Dickhead.

'I art the spy.'

'Nay, nay and a nonny no,' said Dickhead, sounding as if he was singing at the top of his voice. 'Thou art Will the Quill, oft times knowneth as Will the Winker.'

'Yea,' said Will, 'but I am also now Will the Spy.'

Dickhead laughed out loud, and a cloud of blackbirds took off from the common, alarmed by the sudden noise.

''Tis a good one, Will,' he said. 'Thou the king's spy. There is as much chance of thee spying for the king as that of a man walking on the moon.'

'But I am that spy, sire,' Will said. 'I am being paid ten crowns to find the Royal Watcher and to unmask all those who doth produce the *Times*.'

Dickhead's face ran the full gamut of emotions, from shock and horror to despair, and then crumpled as tears rolled down his sallow cheeks.

'But why, Will?' he said in a choked voice that was the quietest it had been since he had been belled. 'How couldst thee? I thought thou were on my side against the king and his corrupteth, rotten regime.'

Now it was Will's turn to laugh. 'Come, dryeth thy tears Dickhead,' he said. 'As if I wouldst turn thee in. We canst have much fun at the king's expense, and also that of his two greedy, grasping advisers Wolsey and Cromwell.'

'How cometh, Will?' asked Dickhead, the sparkle returning to his drying eyes and the full volume to his voice. 'What hath thee in mind, thou rascal of the first order?'

Will whispered his plan so that not a soul on the Common could hear it, not even Claude de Bedsop who was ten yards away disguised as a small tree. In fact he was so well disguised that a passing hound had just stopped and cocked his leg and turned the Frenchman into a reluctant *pissotière*.

Only Dickhead heard Will's scheme, and he laughed so loud that two miles away somebody remarked that it sounded a very common laugh.

Henry VIII was enjoying one of his saner moments in the bar at the Peacock and Partridge. He was wearing his black whiskers, and trying hard to be one of the lads as he swapped Essex wench jokes with the regulars at the inn while quaffing tankards of ale.

The king was passing time waiting for Nell Grinn to finish work and to discuss with him further the possibility of lying on her back for him and allowing him her considerable favours. She had been putting him off for over a week, and now he was becoming more than just a little impatient. Seven minutes was a long time for him normally to wait for a lady's favours. Seven days was definitely worth an entry in the *Genius Book of Records*. The time was fast approaching, he thought, when he would have to order her to do her duty for king and country. He had never been so smitten with a woman, well not for at least ten or so days since he had dallied with that awful sister-in-law of his, Flirty of Flanders.

She had given him him a good time until it came to the matter of what to do to each other in bed. The damned woman had expected him, the King of England, to sucketh her toes. 'Porky hath spoilt thee,' he told her. 'In my bed I am the only one that is sucked.' He had then toe-ended her out of the royal bed.

Henry, ordering up a fifth round of the landlord's finest ale (which tasted much the same as his poorest and was best described as being like dog's pee on the tongue) was unaccustomed to mixing with his subjects, and he did not really know how to conduct himself with ordinary citizens. He had observed them waving and bowing to him from a distance, but it was fascinating to see them in close-up. Amazingly, they seemed fairly decent and not at all the smelly and unclean individuals Wolsey and Cromwell made them out to be. 'All they art good for art their taxes,' said Cromwell.

The king was pleasantly surprised to find that they did not at all seem to mind drinking the ale that he bought them. As at his court, where he was surrounded by professional crawlers and sycophants, he dominated the conversation because nobody was allowed to think let alone speak while he was holding court.

'What 'tis the difference,' Henry said to his companions, 'between courting an Essex wench and fishing in the River Thames?'

'I doth not know,' said sheep farmer Peter Watson, one of the crowd of farmworkers the king was sitting with incognito. 'What 'tis the difference?'

'Thou art less likely to catcheth something nasty in the Thames,' said Henry, roaring with laughter. ''Tis the way I telleth them.'

His new acquaintances dutifully laughed because, although not amusing, the amply built man was clearly well breeched and was not slow to put his hand in his purse. For a free tankard of ale and a glimpse of Nell Grinn's assets as she dipped to serve, Watson and his drinking pals would have laughed all day and all night at the character with the whiskers that seemed to part from his face as he talked.

'Here is one that will slayeth thee,' said Henry, after dipping into his purse for another round. 'Did thou hearest the one about the unmarried Essex wench who was with child? She wenteth home to her father in tears and with swollen stomach, and he sayeth to her, "How doth thy know 'tis yours?"'

More loud laughter, and another round of drinks from Henry. Nell served, dipped and received leering looks from all the company.

'Hath thou heard the one about the young Essex wench who marrieth a very old farmer?' Henry said. 'On their marital night she sayeth, "Oooh, I doth feel that something very strange hath cometh over me." He sayeth, "'Tis old age creeping on."'

More loud laughter, and another round of drinks from Henry and his bottomless purse. Again Nell served, dipped, and as well as the leering looks she also received a sudden grope from Farmer Watson.

'Wench, let me behold thy jugs,' he said. Henry thought he meant her beer tankards, and was aghast when he put the palms of his hands against what she herself described as her 'boiled-over dumplings.'

'Unhand that wench,' said Henry, suddenly boiling over himself – with jealousy and a drink too far.

'Unhand thyself,' said the sheep farmer. 'Thou doth not own her.'

He laughed a loud drunken laugh as he added, 'She liketh farm hands on her, doth Nell.'

Henry was now up on swaying legs. 'Taketh that back or I shalt have thy head off,' he said with a slurred voice.

'Who doth thou thinkst thou art?' said Watson. 'King Henry? No, thou canst be him. He is too busy in his stables mounting his horses.'

There was a bellow of laughter all around, but the king was not laughing. Henry's cheeks turned crimson with rage, lighting up his false black beard. Nobody had ever spoken like that to him throughout his sheltered life. The man would pay for his insolence.

He rushed at Watson and got him in a bear hug. When he did this at court, whoever was grabbed would automatically surrender to the king's great strength.

It was just Henry's luck that on this occasion he had picked on the all-Surrey wrestling champion, a man famous throughout the county for his strength and for carrying two sheep around under his arms. This was the wild man of Walton who had been known to bring tears to a ewe's eyes.

Watson kneed Henry in the breeches to make him break his hold, and then picked him up and whirled him around above his head as easily as if he were a broadsword.

The landlord, Lemmie Pulham, came racing across from the bar to try to intervene but was knocked bandy when the king's feet connected with his head as the sheep farmer spun him like a top.

Watson then suddenly let the giddy Henry go and he sailed across the inn at shoulder height and finished up head first in a barrel of ale. Poorest ale. As the half-conscious king, who had taken yet another heavy bang on the royal noggin, pulled himself out of the barrel, his beard came away.

There was an intake of breath by all the customers that caused a sudden draught as they looked on the bloated, ale-drenched face of their monarch.

''Tis the king,' said Watson. 'The Mad Axeman of Hampton. Quick, away before he getteth his chopper out.'

Watson led the stampede for the door, and the inn was empty by the time Henry had started to recover his senses. Only Pulham, Nell and Claude the Fraud, disguised as an upright chair, were left.

'They didst not mean any harm,' Pulham said to the king, as he sat him down on Claude. The landlord feared that his inn could be closed down, although this was the first trouble there had been at the Peacock and Partridge for all of forty-eight hours.

'Who didst not mean trouble?' asked Henry, frowning.

'The farmer and his hands,' said Pulham.

'Which farmer, which hands?' said the king. 'I knoweth not what thou talketh about.'

'Doth thou knowest me, my liege?' asked Nell.

'I knowest thee not from Adam, nor even Eve,' said

78

the king. 'But I wouldst like to.'

'He hath lost his memory,' said Nell, wiping at the egg-size bruise on the king's forehead with a damp cloth.

'Just as well for Farmer Watson's sake,' said Pulham. 'It hath saved his neck.'

'What shallst we do with him?' said Nell.

'What shallst we do with whom?' slurred the king.

'With thee, thy Majesty,' said Nell. 'We canst not send thee back to the palace in this condition.'

'Palace?' said Henry. 'Which palace? Majesty? Which Majesty? Condition? Which condition?'

Pulham and Nell looked at each other. 'He doth not knowest who he is,' said the landlord. 'There is only one thing I canst do. I shall drive him back to Hampton Court in my cart. Thou, Nell, takest care of the inn.'

As Pulham supported King Henry out of the door, Nell called after him. 'Be careful, father,' she said. 'Take care not to letteth him hath his way with thy horse.'

'Horse?' said Henry. 'What horse?'

It was five hours later when King Henry was found wandering around his maze in a daze. Pulham had dropped him at the Hampton Court gates and then drove off like the wind rather than become involved in an interrogation.

The king staggered groggily into the maze and after wandering around aimlessly stumbled over the footman and the downstairs maid, who were once again giving each other an amazing time.

The footman suddenly became the inchman as he

shrank in fear on looking up from the missionary position into the face of the king. He then dropped into the kneeling position, wondering if the king's chopper would be dropping on to his neck.

'What is this place?' asked the king. 'Who art thou? Who art I?'

The footman and the maid guided their confused monarch back to his private rooms, and Wolsey and Cromwell were summoned along with the king's personal physician, Dr Ivan O'Deah.

'He hath had a blow on the head,' was the confident verdict of the doctor after an hour-long examination.

Wolsey and Cromwell both quietly considered that the large blue and yellow lump on his forehead might have led to that diagnosis just a little quicker.

'Who is this man?' said the king as the doctor inspected him.

'I art thy doctor, Ivan O'Deah. Thou art in safe hands now.'

Wolsey and Cromwell exchanged glances. They reckoned that the doctor's hands were about as safe as a leper's hands holding a runaway bullock. He had only retained his job as the king's personal physician because Henry had given his wife a Royal one some twenty-odd years ago, and she had got him to vow to keep the doctor employed because nobody else would have given him house (or even hospital) room.

Dr O'Deah considered that the cure for just about everything was a tub of ointment and a quick rubdown with a doc leaf. His only other alternative was to amputate, and he took off limbs with the same alacrity that Henry removed heads.

Countless patients had gone to him with common colds and come away minus a limb. He found that it took their mind off the colds. The doctor was convinced his remedies were working because he found that fewer and fewer people were coming to him complaining that they were feeling unwell.

He had developed the rather disconcerting habit of shouting at the top of his voice, 'It's the plague' whenever anybody as much as sniffled in his hearing. It started many a panic during a period in England's history when the plague was often darkening the doorstep.

It was Dr O'Deah who had given the king the most painful experience of his life. He sometimes got a little muddled and gave instructions back to front, and when the king's boils needed to be pricked he managed to tell his assistant to do the reverse.

It was claimed that Henry's screams could be heard for a radius of twenty-five miles, and it would not be an exaggeration to say that the king was boiling mad. The doctor survived with his head intact, thanks to pleas from his wife, but his assistant came under the executioner's axe. In this instance it was not his head that was chopped off.

Dr O'Deah was talked out of amputating one of the king's limbs following his traumatic experience of mixing with his subjects in the Peacock and Partridge. He made do, instead, with smearing some ointment on the bump on the king's head and then ordered Henry to bed in the hope that it would help restore his memory.

Wolsey and Cromwell took over the joint running of the court and the country. Nobody was told about Henry's condition, just that he had got a slight chill. The doctor's cries of 'It's the plague' were largely ignored, although Wolsey and Cromwell both covered their mouths with handkerchiefs just in case.

Queen Marie was given the full story by Claude de Bedsop, and she got word to her cousin, King Francis of France, that if ever he wanted to invade England, now was the time.

But Francis decided against an invasion. He thought it was an English trick. 'I know ze crafty King 'Enri,' he said. ''e 'as not lost 'is memory, just 'is marbles.'

The *Panorama Times* ran the story of the fracas at the inn and Henry's loss of memory in a special one-sheet issue brought out the day after the king had been ordered to bed. They ran the splash under the headline: KING IN ALE-HOUSE BRAWL: LOSES MEMORY.

The Royal Watcher reported on the back page that King Henry was now not only barking mad but no longer knew who he was.

'What hath our great and proud country cometh to,' he wrote, 'when we are runneth by a bestial king who thinketh he is a dog, doth performeth with horses and knowest not neither what day it is nor whoest he is? He hast treated his queen, his latest queen that is, abominably, and now looketh for ways and means to rid himself of her and on to the next conquest. Whilst the king doth layeth on his back wondering in which world he liveth, the two most evil and greedy men in

82

the whole of England, Wolsey and Cromwell, will ruin (rather than run) the country. They wilt doubtless raise taxes to pay for their excesses, and will maketh the most of every minute that the king is incapacitated to filleth their pockets from *your* pockets. How much longer wilt we be prepared to putteth up with their gluttony and their extravagance at our expense?'

Charles Dickhead made an unofficial outside broadcast from the town hall steps at Greenwich. 'Oyez, oyez, oyez,' he shouted. 'Hear ye that His Royal Majesty King Henry hath had the shyte kicked out of him in an ale-house brawl. Now the country is being runneth by two grasping villains. Watcheth thy pockets.'

This was reported back to Wolsey and Cromwell, who were more desperate than ever to get the Royal Watcher's name on the chopping list before he and that accursed *Panorama Times* brought a plague on both their houses.

They doubled Will the Quill's money to twenty golden coins, and Will halved his efforts to find himself but worked double at bringing down the king and his court.

'What king?' asked Henry. 'What court?'

**Will the Winker
A portrait by
Hans Holbein**

There is a tide in the affairs of men
which, taken at the flood,
Can leadeth thee up river or down.
How should I strike now that the King
knoweth not whomest he be?
Should I hold back my plan to maketh
him a laughing stock,
Or shall I turn my spleen on his two evil
advisers?
I shall leave it to the book of fate,
And see what revolutions time bringeth.

84

6

WHILE the king lay in his bed wondering who and where he was, Will caught up with his history book and busied himself on perfecting his latest invention. It consisted of two buckets linked together by a long stretch of chord. He called it his 'yellyphone'. One bucket was in his garret and the other placed down by the front door of the rectory. All any visitor had to do was yell 'Hello' into the downstairs bucket, and Will would reply upstairs.

It was Bernardo who was first to take advantage of the new device. 'Hello!' he yelled into the bucket, following the instructions hand-printed on the side. There was no reply, Will being otherwise detained in the upstairs chamber.

'Hello!' Bernardo called again, and then putting his ear to the bucket as instructed. Still no reply.

For his third attempt, Bernardo placed his head right inside the bucket and yelled 'Hello!'

Success. Will had by now returned to his room and heard the muffled shout coming from his receiver bucket.

'Who doth thou wisheth to speaketh to?' he shouted into his bucket.

'To Will the Quill,' came back the muffled reply.

''Tis I,' said Will. 'Who art thou?'

'Bernardo,' shouted Bernardo at the other end of the line. 'I cometh here from Hampton Court to speaketh to thee on a matter of greateth urgency.'

'Well, it payeth to talketh,' shouted Will. 'Cometh up to my garret. The door is openeth.'

It was another ten minutes before Bernardo appeared in Will's room. He had had great difficulty climbing the stairs because of the slight handicap that the 'yellyphone' bucket was stuck solid on his head and covering his eyes.

The chord had broken when the Reverend Neil Downer had tripped over it on his way to say mass. It was not, however, mass that he said as he tumbled down a flight of stairs. Inside the bucket, it sounded to Bernardo that whoever it was that had gone tumbling past him, had shouted something like, 'Oh, bucket! Thou stupid bastard.'

It took an hour to remove the bucket from Bernardo's head, during which time Will arrived at the conclusion that he would have to go back to the drawing board before trying to patent his project. Possibly, he thought, the world was not yet ready for something as sophisticated as a 'yellyphone'. Perhaps he should concentrate on his other idea, which was to tie a large looking glass around his stomach and walk round with it. Viewers could see moving reflections. He called this his 'bellyvision'.

'What bringeth thou back to my humble abode?' he asked Bernardo after at last pulling off the bucket with the help of some ointment Dr Ivan O'Deah had given him when he had broken a finger a year earlier (O'Deah had offered Will the choice of the ointment or amputation. He had taken the ointment after sticking up two unbroken fingers at the mad doctor).

'I cometh on the instructions of Cardinal Wolsey and Lord Chancellor Cromwell,' he said. 'They wanteth to know how thou fareth with tracking down the Royal Watcher.'

'I senseth that, without a word of a lie, I am in touching distance of him,' said Will. 'But I needeth more time to winneth the confidence of my contact. Meantime I worrieth about my royal book. What news of King Henry? Is the *Panorama Times* correcteth to sayeth that he hath lost his memory?'

Bernardo looked around to make sure nobody could overhear, and he placed the two 'yellyphone' buckets upside down. Only Claude the Fraud, up on the roof, could now hear what was being said.

'Betweenst thee, me and the bedpost,' said Bernardo, ''tis true. The king hath lost his memory. What worrieth me is that Wolsey and Cromwell seeth this as a chance to snatch the throne and shareth power betweenst them.'

'This is a very treasonable thing for thou to sayeth,' said Will, knowing that it was indeed the truth. 'They, after all, hath the ear of the king.'

'Yea, but they wanteth his baubles and his balls as well,' said Bernardo. 'I oweth my loyalty to the king. It is he who tooketh me from the vegetable garden into the Royal court and I satteth on his right hand. It broketh two of his fingers, but he accepteth my humble apologies and he hath listened to me ever since.'

Bernardo leaned closer to Will. 'He hath now lost his reason and his memory,' he confided, 'and there is treachery afoot whilst he layest on the royal bed not knowingest whether he cometh or goeth. Shouldst Wolsey and Cromwell seizeth the throne, I wilt be the first they wilt have beheaded. I hath seen in my crystal eye that they doth mean to have my head off. Then howst wouldst I be able to see into the future?'

'Why doth thou burden me with this knowledge?' asked Will, smelling a sewer rat.

'Because, Will, thou, liketh me, hath complete loyalty and allegiance to the king,' he said. 'He wouldst not hath trusteth thee with assisting with his biography unless he knewest thou were an honest and honourable subject who wouldst be prepareth to lay down thy life for him.'

'Wow, wow, wowest thee!' said Will, 'Thou must not taketh too much for granted. I wilt willingly layeth down some words on parchment for the king, but my life? Thou must be jesting. I couldst not do that for the life of me.'

'I was hoping that thou wouldst joineth me in a plot against Wolsey and Cromwell,' said Bernardo. 'In the name of Henry the Magnificent.'

'As long as 'tis nothing that would risketh my neck,' said Will. 'My ruff wouldst be lost without it.'

'I just needeth to knowest that I can calleth on thee,' said Bernardo. 'If, as I believeth, those two dastardly scoundrels are planning to seizeth power while the king lieth abed without knowledge of whomst he is, then it is the duty of we loyal subjects to fighteth for him. For our king and for our country. Canst I count on thee, Will?'

'Yea, you mayst count on me,' said Will, crossing his

fingers and thinking quietly to himself that, for Henry, he hoped that it would be the final count.

The 'yellyphone' chord had been repaired, and the call-and-answer buckets were back in place as Will returned to his history of England. He had reached the Battle of Hastings in 1066, and described in gory detail the demise of King Harold. Despite what previous historians had written, Will revealed in his no-holds-barred style that Harold 'didst not dieth from an arrow in the eye but from a Norman lance uppeth his arse.'*

Will was determined in his walk through English history to take away any glory that kings and queens were claiming because he knew that most facts had been twisted in their favour by what were known as the 'Royal Spin' doctors. Will could provide more spin than a witch's spinning wheel. Doubtless, he thought, Henry's spin doctors would try to make him the patron saint of marriage, while in truth he was the patron sinner of divorce.

He was startled out of his spinning train of thought by a call on his yellyphone.

''Ello, 'ello,' came the unmistakeable voice of Queen Marie.

Will put his hand over the top of his bucket so that Marie could not hear him. 'What on earth doth that old French tart wanteth?' he said aloud.

*A new interpretation of the Bayeux Tapestry has long since shattered the myth that Harold died after being hit by an arrow in the eye. The myth was originated by a Norman historian who made a wrong identification when studying the battle scene on the tapestry. It is considered more likely that Harold was chopped down by four Norman knights after being toppled from his horse by a lance thrust.

'Hello, who doth thou wisheth to speak to?' he shouted into the bucket.

''Ello, 'ello,' came the response.

'Hello, who doth thou wanteth?' Will shouted.

''Ello, 'ello,' was all he got.

'Putteth thy ear to the bucket, you sillieth old trout,' he yelled.

''Ello, 'ello,' came the reply.

Will kicked the bucket in frustration, and ran to the window. He climbed out on to the roof and looked down in some astonishment at Queen Marie, who was, perhaps fittingly, dressed up as an old hag. Will felt that the diamond-studded crown on her head rather scuttled the idea of the disguise. The queen, crouched over the bucket, gave a royal wave as she spotted him.

'Putteth thy ear to the bucket,' he shouted, and then returned to his receiver.

''Tis Will the Quill here,' he said into the bucket. 'Doth thou wanteth to speaketh to me?'

All Will could hear was a mumble. He clambered back on to the roof. 'Putteth thy ear to the bucket whenst thou listeneth and thy lips to the bucket whenst thou talketh,' he shouted, his right eye on the blink.

The queen smiled up at him, showing teeth blacked out with coal dust.

He went back to his receiver. 'What canst I do for thee, your Majesty?' he asked at the top of his voice.

'I wisheth to speak to zee on a matter most urgent,' she said. 'Canst I come up ze stairs?'

'The door is openeth,' said Will. 'Please cometh up.'

Marie was puffing like an old carthorse when she

finally arrived at the garret after climbing the twelve flights of stairs in flimsy, golden shoes that looked out of place beneath the black sackcloth dress she wore to camouflage her standing as the Queen of England.

'How doth zee climbeth ze stairs every day?' she asked, fighting to regain her breath as she sat on the upturned yellyphone bucket, the only seat that Will could offer. He was not inclined to give up the chair at his table because she would have been in a position to stick her French nose into his English history book. She would not have been best pleased to see his description of French King Louis VI, who was known to friends and enemies alike as Fatty. Describing his defeat by England's Henry I at the Battle of Brémule, Will wrote, 'King Louis was so fat that his entire battalion hiddeth behind him. The army didst marcheth on his stomach.'

'To what doth I owe this honour, Your Majesty?' Will asked the queen, who had now regained her breath and composure, although her witch's hat beneath the crown and the blackened teeth robbed her of any regal bearing.

She waved her heavily-fingered hands at him. 'Shoosh, *mon cherie*,' she said, taking time to decide which one of her fingers to put to her lips. 'Nobody must know zat I am 'ere. I 'ave come to asketh zee a *grande* favour.'

'I am your humble servant,' said Will, bowing his head.

'As ze Royal Watcher, thou wilt know zat mon 'usband is badly wounded, perhaps mortally, *non*?'

Will forced a laugh, his right eye going into such a rapid wink that it looked permanently closed.

'I don't zink zee shouldst laugheth at ze situation,'

said Marie. 'After all, 'e is ze King of England, alzough I too 'ave to admit zat I findeth 'is all *très* funny.'

'No, no, hey nonny no,' said Will, borrowing a denial style from Charles Dickhead. 'I laugheth not at the serious condition of King Henry, but at thy calling me the Royal Watcher. As if I were he! Why, thy husband would hath my head off my shoulders in the blinking of an eye.'

Queen Marie showed her blackened teeth as she gave a knowing smile. 'Monsieur Will,' she said, 'I 'ave a better information service zan mon 'usband. Claude de Bedsop is ze finest spy in ze whole of Europe. Even as we speaketh, he is under ze bed of ze king in case zer should be any developments. Your secret is safe wiz me, but in return I wanteth your cooperation.'

The queen's black teeth suited her blackmailing technique.

'What doth thou wanteth of me,' said a resigned Will, his eye blinking a little less frantically.

'If my 'usband, 'ow you say, kicks ze bucket,' she said, rapping her fourteen fingers on the bucket on which she sat. 'I want you to campaign for me in ze much read and respected *Times* to become ze ruling Queen of England and not just ze decoration zat I am at present.'

'That canst be done,' said Will, lying through his teeth. As if England wanted a froggie, a female froggie at that, on the English throne.

'*Bon*,' said Marie, holding up two of her famous fingers. 'Just deux more things. I want thou to keepeth an eye, not ze blinking one, on zose wicked men Wolsey, Cromwell and Bernardo. Zey will be looking to 'ave my 'ead off if my 'usband snuffs it. If zis is so, you must expose zem in ze *Times* and point out zat my cousin, King Francis of France, will cometh over and give zem a *très bon* kick in ze derrière.'

'I wilt watcheth the situation carefully,' said Will. 'Now thou sayeth *two* more things. What is the other one?'

'Thou driveth me wild wiz your flirty winking,' said Marie, lifting her black dress and revealing her royal jewels. 'Taketh me now and giveth me 'appenis.'

She made a grab for Will's private parts with her fourteen fingers. He had never been under such heavy-handed attack.

Will was about to lie back and think of *entente cordial* when he was saved by the sudden sound of a disembodied voice.

'Hello. Is there anybody there? Oooh, stop mucking about and answer me.'

The voice was coming from the bucket on which the queen had been sitting, and it clearly belonged to the Lord Chancellor, Thomas Cromwell.

The queen looked around in terror. She thought Cromwell was in the room.

'Don't worryeth,' said Will, 'he is downstairs at the front door.'

'But 'e must not see me 'ere,' said the queen. ''e would 'ave my 'ead. How canst I avoideth him?'

'Here,' said Will, pointing above Marie's head. 'Out of the window.'

'Ze window?' said Marie. 'But we're uppeth in ze roof .'

'Climbeth down the drainpipe and the ivy,' said Will.

'Ze drainpipe and ze ivy?' said Marie, making it sound like a Christmas carol. 'But I am ze Queen of England. I cannot do such a zing. I could falleth and breaketh my neck. Zen what will becometh of me?'

Will thought quickly. 'Hideth thy crown under thy dress,' he said, 'and walketh casually down the stairs as if thou art the cleaning skivvy going home.'

A petrified Queen Marie did what she was told, while Will answered the yellyphone.

'Hello,' he said, 'Who doth thou wanteth to talk to?'

'Hello, is Will the Quill in?' shouted Cromwell.

''Tis I who speaketh,' said Will.

''Tis Cromwell, Lord Chancellor here,' came the reply. 'I wanteth to speaketh to thee on a matter of greateth urgency.'

'Cometh on up,' said Will. 'The door is openeth.'

Cromwell was puffing like an old bull when he arrived at the garret. He was shown to the bucket seat.

'I doth not thinketh much of thy taste,' he said between wheezing breaths.

'I quite like the room,' said Will, looking around the squashed garret in which you could not have swung a tailless cat.

'I meaneth thy taste in women,' said Cromwell. 'That hag I passeth on the stairs. Thou couldst not payeth me to giveth her one. Were thou not putteth off by that crown-shape hump on her back?'

'She cleaneth up for me,' said Will. 'I wouldst not touch her with a punting pole.'

Cromwell had recovered his breath. 'Nice place thou

hath here,' he said, glancing round the room which took all of three seconds. 'Comfortably small. Believeth me, I envyeth thee. The seven hundred and fifty rooms I hath in my palace taketh a lot to upkeepeth.'

Will moved uncomfortably on his seat. He knew that Cromwell had not come to talk about being envious of his humble home.

'Thou honourest me with thy presence,' lied Will. 'Now, what canst I do for thee, sire?'

''Tis a most delicate matter I wisheth to discusseth with thee,' said Cromwell, peering around for any sign of an eavesdropper. Even Bedsop was missing. 'Hath thou heard about the king's condition?'

'I heareth only that he has a chill,' lied Will.

''Tis much more serious than that,' said Cromwell. 'Not to putteth too strongeth a point on it, he hath knocked himself silly. Or shouldst I say sillier.'

'My heart grievest,' lied Will.

'What worrieth me,' said Cromwell, talking in a conspiratorial tone, 'is that shouldst he not maketh a full recovery that cunning, conniving Cardinal Wolsey hath designs on the throne.'

'Nay, thou doth not say,' said Will, trying to think how he should arrange his face. Should he show sympathy? Fear? Shock? Despair? He decided on a straight face. 'But what canst a poor scribbler like I doeth about it?'

'If the worst comes to the worst, God forbid, and the king croaketh it,' said Cromwell, 'thou canst becomst a powerful ally to me.'

'To thee?' said Will, trying not to let his mask slip to

reveal incredulity. 'But how, pray?'

'Thou canst useth your contacts at the British Broadcasting Criers organisation to help getteth me the right image,' said Cromwell. 'The criers can shouteth my praises around the towns and shires, and thou canst useth your talents with the quill to write articles about me that wilt flattereth me and showest me up to be a born leader. Which, of course, I doth be.'

'And in return?' said Will, playing the Chancellor's game.

'In return...' said Cromwell, his eyes narrowing, his nostrils flaring and his voice going up an octave, '... in return I shall giveth thee a dukedom if I becometh the new ruler. Cromwell, King of England.'

'Will the Quill, Duke of Stratford East,' said Will, playing along.

'Then thou wilt sidest with me?' said Cromwell. 'Wilt thou Will?'

Will nodded and was about to ask for the offer of the dukedom in writing when the voice of Cardinal Wolsey came loud and clear from between Cromwell's legs.

'Hello. Hello. Doth there be any soul at home?' he was shouting into the downstairs bucket.

What little colour Cromwell had in his face drained away. 'I'm doomed,' he said, suffering a panic attack. 'D-o-o-m-e-d, I tell thee. Wolsey will have my head if he findeth out that I plotteth against him. How canst I avoideth him?'

'Here,' said Will, pointing above the Chancellor's head. 'Out of the window.'

'The window?' said the Lord Chancellor. 'But we're

1. King Henry (Sidney James, second left) holds court with Cardinal Wolsey (Terry Scott, right), Thomas Cromwell (Kenneth Williams, left) and Sir Roger de Lodgerley (Charles Hawtrey).

2. King Henry (Sidney James, right) gets a lesson in 'le chat' from the King of France (Peter Gilmore).

3. Queen Marie (Joan Sims) looks on as King Henry tries to out-plot Lord Hampton of Wick (Kenneth Connor).

4. The plot thickens as Thomas Cromwell (Kenneth Williams) conspires with Guy Fawkes (Bill Maynard, right) and Lord Hampton of Wick (Kenneth Connor, centre). *BFI Stills*

5. King Henry (Sidney James) wonders if Thomas Cromwell (Kenneth Williams, left), Sir Roger de Lodgerley (Charles Hawtrey, second left) and Cardinal Wolsey (Terry Scott, right) are as loyal as they pretend to be. *BFI Stills*

6. Queen Marie (Joan Sims) listens to Cardinal Wolsey (Terry Scott) embroidering a plot. *BFI Stills*

7. The cunning, conniving Cardinal Wolsey (Terry Scott) and the shifty, scheming Thomas Cromwell (Kenneth Williams) are royally surprised. *BFI Stills*

8. A rather over eager Thomas Cromwell (Kenneth Williams) awaits the signature of the King (Sidney James).

9. Thomas Cromwell (Kenneth Williams) and Sir Roger de Lodgerley (Charles Hawtrey) wonder about a poison chalice for King Henry (Sidney James). *BFI Stills*

10. Queen Marie (Joan Sims) advances on Thomas Cromwell (Kenneth Williams) who responds: 'Ooooh, stop mucking

11. Sir Roger de Lodgerley (Charles Hawtrey) points the finger at King Henry (Sidney James), but it's his neck that will be on the block. *BFI Stills*

12. Necks please! Thomas Cromwell (Kenneth Williams) and Cardinal Wolsey (Terry Scott) join King Henry's chopping

uppeth in the roof.'

'Climbeth down the drainpipe and the ivy,' said Will.

'The drainpipe? The ivy?' said Cromwell, his voice breaking. 'But I hath no head for heights. My nose bleedeth when I getteth uppeth on a horse.'

Will thought quickly. He snatched the cloth off his table. 'Goeth down on thy knees,' he said.

Cromwell's eyes were spinning with hysteria. 'On my knees?' he said. 'Now? 'Tis not the time for that sort of thing. Maybe another day...'

Will pushed him down, and draped the cloth around him like a cape. He bunched one end of it up around his face so that his features were hidden. 'Now goeth down the stairs on thy knees,' he said. 'If thou passeth Wolsey keepeth thy head down, and pretendeth to clean the stairs. Let him think that thou art the cleaning skivvy.'

As the fearful Cromwell started down the stairs on his knees, Will shouted into the bucket. 'Sorryeth to hath kept thee waiting,' he said. 'Will the Quill here. Who doth calleth?'

''Tis I, Wolsey,' shouted the Cardinal. 'I wanteth to speaketh to thee on a matter of greateth urgency.'

'Cometh on up,' said Will. 'The door is openeth.'

Wolsey, a much larger man than Cromwell, was as purple as his cassock when he arrived at the garret. He collapsed on to the bucket seat.

'I doth not thinketh much of thy taste,' he said as he fought for his breath.

'I quite like the room,' said Will, thinking he had had this conversation before.

'I meaneth thy taste in women,' said Wolsey. 'That hag I passeth on the stairs. She looketh a dwarf woman. Thou obviously liketh them small. She appeareth for all the world like Cromwell's mother. I always knew he cometh from low-class stock, but he giveth all those airs and graces just because he passeth one or two law exams.'

'The woman you speaketh of doth cleaneth up for me,' said Will. 'I wouldst not touch her with a punting pole.'

Wolsey had recovered his breath. 'Nice place thou hath here,' he said, as if reading from Cromwell's script. 'Comfortably small. Believeth me, I envyeth thee. It doth remindeth me of the little place I builteth for myself at Hampton Court which was my home until the king took it off me as a sop during one of his sulks.'

Will moved uncomfortably on his seat. He knew that Wolsey, like Cromwell, had not come to talk about being envious of his humble home.

'Thou honourest me with thy presence,' lied Will. 'Now, what canst I do for thee, sire?'

''Tis a most delicate matter I wisheth to discusseth with thee,' said Wolsey, peering around, as did Cromwell, for any sign of an eavesdropper. 'Hath thou heard about the king's condition?'

'I heareth only that he has a chill,' lied Will again.

''Tis much more serious than that,' said Wolsey. 'Not to putteth too strongeth a point on it, he hath knocked himself silly. Or shouldst I say sillier.'

'My heart still grievest,' lied Will again.

'*Still* grievest?' said Wolsey.

'Ay,' said Will, trying to think of what to say next. 'I

hath grieveth since I heardest that the king hath a chill. Dr O'Deah hath given the impression that it might be the plague. It hath caused a hold-up with the book.'

'Dr O'Deah hath no idea what day it is,' said Wolsey. 'As for the book, thou canst put that aside. The king also doth not know what day it is, nor what night.'

Will guessed what was coming next.

'What worrieth me,' said Wolsey, talking in a conspiratorial tone, 'is that shouldst the king not maketh a full recovery that cunning, conniving Chancellor Cromwell hath designs on the throne.'

'Nay, thou doth not say,' said Will, hoping his face was not mirroring the predictability of it all. 'But what canst a poor scribbler like I doeth about it?'

'If the worst comes to the worst, God forbid, and the king goeth to the great kingdom in the sky,' said Wolsey, making a huge sign of the cross with a raised finger and looking heavenward, 'you canst becomst a powerful ally to me.'

'To thee?' said Will, trying not to show that he had been here, done this. 'But how, pray?'

'Thou canst use your contacts at the British Broadcasting Criers organisation to help getteth me an even better image than I own now,' said Wolsey, deviating just a little from the Cromwell line. 'The criers can shouteth my praises around the towns and shires, and you canst use your talents with the quill to write articles about me that wilt showeth me off in the best possible light as the right man to sitteth on the throne of England.'

Will decided he needed to change his own script. 'But

is there not something in our constitution about right of ascension and the royal line? Is there not a legitimate heir to the throne?'

'Piddlecock!' exclaimed Wolsey. 'The king hath sired many bastard children, but the only ones with a proper claim to the throne art a sickly boy called Edward, and two weakling girls, Mary and Elizabeth. As if either of them couldst make a monarch. Pah! A queen on the throne, I ask thee! And anyway, who canst be sure that this Elizabeth has proper royal blood in her veins? Her mother, Anne Boleyn, putteth it about so much that she were knowneth as Anne of the Thousand Lays.'

'What about the king's brother?' asked Will.

The Cardinal let out a bellowing laugh. 'What, Porky?' he said, almost choking with merriment. 'And hath his wife Flirty as queen. Doeth me a favour.'

He looked up from his bucket seat with determination glinting in his eyes. 'Nay, Will, lad,' he said, 'with thy help I wouldst rewrite the constitution and I wouldst take over as king until such times as a more acceptable male heir couldst be found. I might even produceth a few myself with the ladies that I wouldst inviteth into the royal bed. You, Will, can helpeth me.'

'Helpeth thee sire an heir, sire?'

'Nay, thou canst use thy word power to giveth me the right standing with the citizens of this great country.'

'And in return?' said Will, playing the Cardinal's game.

'In return...' said Wolsey, crossing himself and also Will, '...in return I shall maketh thee chief cardinal if I becometh the new ruler. Wolsey, King of England.'

100

'Will the Quill, Cardinal in chief,' said Will, playing along.

'Then thou wilt sidest with me?' said Wolsey. 'Wilt thou, Will?'

Will nodded and was about to ask for the offer of the Cardinalship in writing when a voice came loud and clear from between Wolsey's legs.

'Hello. Hello. May the Lord be with you,' came the disembodied voice in the bucket.

Cardinal Wolsey fell on his fat knees. 'I hear thee, my Lord,' he said, his hands pressed together and his eyes shut tight. 'Please helpeth me become ruler of all England and, in particular, the treasury.'

'Hello. Hello. Can thou helpeth me?' was the response.

'Helpeth thee?' said the Cardinal, still in a praying position. 'But it is thee that I needeth to help me. Please telleth me that thou wilt giveth me the key to the kingdom.'

'Hello. Hello. I've losteth the key. Canst thou helpest me get in?'

'Thou hath losteth the key to the kingdom?' said the Cardinal, his eyes popping wide open.

'That's deareth old Reverend Neil Downer,' said Will. 'He's always losing the key to the rectory. Perhaps you could be so kindeth as to openeth the door to him on your way out.'

'But I must not be seeneth here by a member of my church,' said Wolsey in a sudden panic. 'He mighteth realiseth that I am uppeth to no good and reporteth me to the king. The priests and monks doth not like me just because I shutteth down the monasteries and I hath all the power and the glory. How canst I avoideth him?'

'Here,' said Will, pointing above the Cardinal's head. 'Out of the window.'

'The window?' said the Cardinal. 'But we're uppeth in the roof.'

''Tis the only way apart from the stairs,' said Will.

'Then the roof it is,' said the Cardinal. 'Giveth me a bunk up.'

'What, here?' said Will, jesting. 'Now?'

'No time for that sort of thing,' said the Cardinal. 'On the morrow perhaps. Help me up on to thy roof.'

And so it was that the huge and mighty Cardinal Wolsey got himself stuck in the window of a garret in Tower Hamlets.

It took Will, the Reverend Neil Downer, the local blacksmith and a liberal spreading of Dr O'Deah's ointment two hours to free him.

As he dropped back down into the garret, making the entire rectory shudder, the Cardinal made the sign of the cross and left in a purple huff.

Will was sitting thinking back over the day's confusing events, and trying to get his concentration on his history of England. He turned to his parchment and was just describing how 'William the Conker was so calleth because he hath a big conk' when his scratching of the quill was interrupted by the yellyphone.

'Oyez, oyez, oyez,' came the unmistakeable voice of Charles Dickhead, who hardly needed a yellyphone. 'Hear ye that I am downstairs waiting to cometh up.'

'Cometh on up,' shouted Will. 'The door is openeth.'

Dickhead had come with tidings that he had overheard at the BBC. 'There is deep concern over the king's worsening condition,' he shouted. 'The bump he gotteth on his head during the brawl at the Peacock and Partridge hath made him even sillier than usual. We must getteth out another special edition of the *Times*. There hath never been such interest. We selleth out of all two hundred and fifteen copies of the last issue.'

Dickhead was shouting so loudly that the whole of Tower Hamlets heard the news as it boomed from the downstairs bucket. Will realised what was happening and cut the cord connecting the two buckets. It was the first known instance of a phone being disconnected.

'Thou wilt not believe the day I hath had,' said Will. 'I am involved in more plots than there are in a graveyard.'

He started to recount them. 'Bernardo wisheth me to joineth his plot against Wolsey and Cromwell,' he said, noting it down. 'Queen Marie wisheth me to joineth her plot against Wolsey, Cromwell and Bernardo. Cromwell wisheth me to joineth his plot against Wolsey, who in turn wisheth me to joineth his plot against Cromwell. And we, Dickhead, hath a plot against them all. Verily, 'tis a plot within a plot.'

Over at Hampton Court, King Henry overheard Cromwell and Wolsey discussing in which plot they would bury him.

'Plot?' he said. 'What plot?'

**Will the Winker
A portrait by
Hans Holbein**

Methinks there are plots afoot to maketh
the King regret not so much dying, but
the very act of being born.
With compatriots like Cromwell and the
cunning Wolsey, who needeth enemies?
What causeth me great disturbance
is that though I have the inclination
I mayst not have the time to strike
Before Henry the Mediocre
Becomes worm meat beneath the sod
in what wouldst be the final final plot.

7

THERE were good tidings and there were bad tidings from Hampton Court. The BBC criers delivered regular bulletins on Henry's health, broadcasting from town hall steps across the land as the citizens of England waited with overwhelming apathy for news of their king. The good tidings, although not to all ears, were that King Henry was now well enough to get up and carry on ruling the country. The bad tidings were kept from all but a select few at the Court.

It was his personal valet who first realised all was not right. 'Bringeth me my ballroom gown with the bell-shaped skirt, my gold high-heeled shoes and my lace underskirts,' were the first words the king spoke to him as he came out of a deep sleep.

'I beggeth thy pardon, thy Royal Highness?' said the valet.

'Thou heardest me, numskull,' said Henry. 'What on earth doth a queen have to do to getteth the clothes that she wanteth. Cometh thee on, moveth thyself or I wilt squeeze thy testicles until thy eyes watereth.'

Wolsey and Cromwell rushed to the king's bedroom when told of his behaviour. They found him sitting in front of a mirror applying rouge to his cheeks.

'What art thou doing?' asked Wolsey. ''Tis no way for a King of England to behaveth.'

'Art thou addressing me?' Henry said in a high-pitched effeminate voice, shooting a withering look at

Wolsey. 'How dareth thee addresseth me in that manner. As Queen of England I demandeth proper respect or thy head wilt be at thy feet.'

'We art just concerned that perhaps thou are not, uh, feeling thyself, thy Majesty,' said Cromwell.

'Feeling myself?' screamed Henry. 'Feeling myself? What doth thou taketh me for. Some sort of pervert? I can getteth any one of a thousand thousand men to cometh and feeleth me if I so wisheth.'

'Shouldst thou perhaps consider returning to thy bed?' said Wolsey, pulling down the covers of the Royal four-poster.

'Thou dirty old beast!' spat Henry. 'Thou wanteth to getteth me between the Royal sheets and hath thy way with the Queen of England. As England's premier cardinal, thou shouldst be ashamed of thyself.'

'Perhaps a glass of mead will help thee feel better,' said Cromwell, thinking how they could slip a potion into it to put the king to sleep for a spell.

'Thou must thinketh I was born yesterday,' said the king. 'Doth thou truly believeth that I would sup any drink prepareth by thee? All thee men art the same. Thou wanteth to getteth a girl in a stupor so that she will not sayeth no. Well I not only sayeth "no" but also telleth thee to getteth thy testicles into knots.'

Wolsey and Cromwell bowed their way out of the bedroom, both wondering what constituted madness in the eyes of the law.

Dr Ivan O'Deah was sent for, and after examining Henry in the privacy of his bedroom he came out looking shaky yet elated.

'The bad tidings,' he reported to Wolsey and Cromwell, 'are that his Majesty thinketh he is Queen Henrietta.'

''Tis quite preposterous,' said Wolsey. 'And, pray, why art thou looking so pleased with thyself?'

'He hath asketh me to marry him,' said Dr O'Deah. 'Thou gazeth upon the next King of England.'

'Over my dead body,' said Wolsey.

'If needs be,' said Dr O'Deah, already feeling his power.

'What doth thou prescribeth?' asked Cromwell.

'Ointment to be spread over his bosom twice a day,' said O'Deah. ''Tis treatment that I wilt administereth personally.'

'But how wilt that cureth him?' said Wolsey, quietly making up his mind that the doctor had to go regardless of any hold he had over the king... or queen.

'It wilt not cureth him,' said the mad doctor. 'But it wilt helpeth hasten his sexual transformation and bringeth nearer the day of our marriage. Our union wilt be celebrated throughout the land.'

'And what, pray, about Mrs O'Deah?' asked Cromwell. 'We all knowst she had a fling with the king.'

'She mayst come to the wedding,' said Dr O'Deah. 'Now I must away to arrange my divorce and the calling of the banns.'

The doctor had not been gone for more than thirty seconds before he was arrested by guards on the instructions of Cardinal Wolsey, and thrown into the Tower on a charge of trying to unlawfully convert the King of England.

107

Wolsey and Cromwell were poring over the Magna Carta to see if it covered the eventuality of a sex-change monarch when 'Henrietta' swept into the room wearing one of Queen Marie's long skirts that came just above his knees. His cheeks and lips were covered in rouge that had just missed their targets, so that his lips looked twice as big as usual.

'Listeneth to me Wolsey,' he said in a voice that had risen an octave and had a pronounced vibrato. 'I am the only one that is alloweth to weareth a dress. I doth not want to seeth thee in a gown again or it wilt be off with thy head. Is that quite understoodeth?'

'Yea, sire... ma'am,' said Wolsey, straightening his cassock and thinking to himself that he much preferred the king as a barking dog than a demented old queen.

'Right, to business,' said Henrietta. 'I wanteth thou to draw up a decree that from this day forth all English women will have equal rights in the eyes of the law and equal employment rights.'

Wolsey and Cromwell exchanged glances. Now they *knew* the king had gone mad.

Will the Quill sat in his garret wondering how he should best describe the reign of Henry I for his true, unexpurgated history of England. Henry, the youngest son of William the Conqueror, had fathered no fewer than twenty illegitimate children.*

'Henry I,' wrote Will in his blunt, no-frills style, 'was neither the first, nor certainly the last, King of England

---

*Henry I, fourth son of William the Conqueror, reigned from 1100 to 1135. He fathered twenty-two children, but only two of them were legitimate.

to be ruled by his balls rather than his brains. He spent so much time with extra-curricular affairs rather than affairs of the State that he became known as Henry the Shagger. Any historian studying his reign would have to cometh to the conclusion that he screwed up.'

Will was startled by a sudden 'psst!' sound emanating from the yellyphone bucket. 'Will, art thou there?' came a whispering voice. ''Tis I, Bernardo. I needeth to speaketh to thee on a matter most urgent.'

'The door is openeth,' said Will. 'Please cometh up.'

Bernardo was carrying the downstairs bucket with him when he arrived, breathless, at the room at the top.

'Why doth thou carryeth the receiver?' said Will.

'Because is it imperative that we are not overheardeth by the Royal Watcher,' said Bernardo. 'The latest events at the palace are such that they could bringeth about the fall of the king and queen, or rather the queen and queen.'

'What on earth doth thou meanst, Bernardo?' said Will. 'Thou talketh with twisted tongue.'

Bernardo described the king's latest exhibition, stating among other things that by wearing Queen Marie's too-short gown, he had created a new fashion, the money-skirt. 'Surely,' said Will, 'mini-skirt would be a more fitting description.'

'Oh nay,' said Bernardo, peering into his glass eye, ''tis the money-skirt rather than mini-skirt because I seeth that whoever doth createth it will maketh a fortune.'

'Why cometh to me about this crisis?' asked Will, wondering if anybody would believe it if he printed it

109

in his Royal Watcher column.

'Thou must cometh to Hampton Court and intervieweth the king for the book,' said Bernardo. ''Tis important that this development doth becometh a matter of historical record, and it wilt stoppeth Wolsey and Cromwell from taking the throne away from His, I mean Her, Majesty. Even as we speaketh, they are plotting to have him putteth into the Tower.'

'On what grounds?' asked Will.

'They sayeth that he hath disgraced the throne, although Henry insists that he doth now graceth it,' said Bernardo. 'Pray cometh, bringeth your quill and writeth a book that could saveth the king's neck.'

'I wilt cometh without further ado,' said Will, keen to get inside information for his *Times* column on what appeared to be the fall of the House of Tudor. He wondered how *Henrietta the Magnificent* would work as a book title.

As they came downstairs, they met the Reverend Neil Downer on his way up.

'Hath thou heardst the news?' he said, blessing them both.

'What news is that, Reverend?' said Will, giving him the full time of day because he was six months behind with the rent.

''Tis His Majesty the King,' said Reverend Downer, 'he hath been converted.'

'Where didst thou hearest that?' asked a shocked Bernardo.

''Tis the talk of my congregation,' said the priest. 'It seemeth that he hath crossed over.'

110

'Crossed over?' said Bernardo. 'What meaneth thou?'

'The rumour from Hampton Court is that the king hath converted to a strange new religion in which instead of making the sign of the cross he doth cross dresses,' said the priest. 'This couldst be very grave news for the Church. We hath only just gotteth used to being the Church of England. Now it seemeth we wilt becometh the church of cross-dressers rather than cross-bearers.'

Meantime, Claude the Fraud was giving a full report to Queen Marie on the extraordinary events in the east wing of Hampton Court. He had been hiding under the king's bed when he heard him ordering his valet to dress him in the queen's clothes. It was the first time his heart had warmed to the King of England.

'What doth zee meaneth 'Enrietta is ze new queen of England?' screeched Queen Marie. '*I* am ze queen of England. Who is zis pretender to my throne?'

''Enri, thy 'usband,' said Claude.

''Enri, my 'usband?' said Marie, her voice going up several decibels. ''ow can zis be? 'e is more man zan any man I knoweth.'

'Not any more,' said Claude. ''e 'as decided to cometh out of ze closet. From now on 'e will be knowneth as 'Enrietta, Queen of England.'

'But 'ow doth zat leaveth me,' said Marie. ''ow would 'e liketh it if I suddenly put on his breeches and called myself ze king?'

''e would choppeth off thy penis,' said Claude. 'Zere is only one zing to do. Thou must letteth ze great British public knoweth what is 'appening. Letteth zem chooseth

111

between zee and ze mad king who zinks 'e is a queen.'

'Zat is good zinking,' said Marie. 'I shalt pay anuzzer visit to ze Royal Watcher. 'e will write an article in ze *Times* zat putteth me in ze good light or I wilt tell 'Enri zat 'e is 'is biggest enemy, ze Watcher.'

'Thou meanest zat thou wilt tell 'Enrietta,' said Claude. ''Enri wilt not answer to any uzzer name.'

Claude secretly envied 'Enri/'Enrietta. He had always wanted to be known as Claudette, but society was not yet ready to accept that there were men who preferred to be women. Queen 'Enrietta could change public thinking by his/her bold stand.

Will the Quill was fighting to keep a straight face as he sat listening to King Henry, alias Queen Henrietta, explaining 'her' new outlook on life. He was sitting alongside his four-poster bed wearing a nice little lace number that Queen Marie had brought over with her from Paris. The hem of the skirt did not even reach Henry's hairy knees.

'I wanteth my book to reflecteth the new England,' said Henry/Henrietta. 'I wanteth to introduceth a fairer society in which women are not treated as second-class citizens. They wilt getteth equal pay, we shalt hath women doctors, women teachers and women priests.'

Will tried not to explode with laughter. Women priests? Whatever next!

'How, thy Royal Highness,' asked Will, 'doth I explaineth to thy subjects that thou art no longer King Henry but hath now becometh Queen Henrietta?'

'What doth thou meaneth?' said Henry/Henrietta. 'I

112

never hath heard of this King Henry.'

'But thou hath a wife, Queen Marie,' said Will.

'How dareth thou speaketh to thy queen in such a manner,' said Henry/Henrietta. 'I wouldst order that your head be cutteth off were it not for the fact that I findeth thou extraordinarily attractive. Thy cheeky wink doth driveth me wild. Wouldst thou taketh my hand in marriage and becometh my king?'

'But I thought thou were promised to the doctor,' said Will, wondering how he could dig himself out of this hole.

'I wilt issue a decree that will alloweth English women to practise polygamy,' said Henry/Henrietta. 'They will hath as many husbands as they wish. Now, what sayeth thee to my proposal?'

'I am already promised to another,' said Will defensively, his right eye blinking at top speed.

'Well unpromise thyself,' ordered Henry/Henrietta, making a sudden grab for Will's private parts.

Will was just about to be forced to lie back on the four-poster bed and think of England when Wolsey and Cromwell entered the room with a detail of guards. 'Arresteth him immediately, and taketh him to the Tower,' ordered Wolsey.

Two guards snatched Will from either side, and started to force him towards the door. A terrified Will wondered who had exposed him as being the Royal Watcher.

'Not him, thou imbeciles,' said Wolsey. 'The one in the dress.'

'But this is our king,' said the guards captain.

Henry/Henrietta stamped her foot. 'I am thy queen,

thou silly man,' he said. 'Art thou blind or something?'

'Thou art not our king?' said the captain.

'Doth I look like a king?' said Henry/Henrietta, pouting his rouged lips.

That clinched it for the captain. 'All right guards,' he ordered. 'Arresteth this imposter.'

Will, watching what were historic events with a gaping mouth, was surprised at the tame surrender of the king/queen. The guards had to chase him/her only four times around the four-poster bed before they overpowered him/her and led the muddled monarch off to the Tower.

While Wolsey and Cromwell squabbled over which of them was now in charge of running the country, Will hurried back to his garret to write the Royal Watcher's report of events for a special issue of the *Panorama Times*. He was astonished to find Queen Marie, in her hag's disguise, waiting for him in his room.

'Ah, *mon cheri*,' she said, frightening the life out of him as she rose from the bucket seat in her black sackcloth dress. 'I 'ope thou doth not mindeth my 'aving let myself in. Ze nice priest downstairs sayeth I could waiteth 'ere for thy return.'

'It wouldst have been easier to talketh to me at Hampton Court,' said Will, getting over the initial shock of finding her haunting his home. 'I hath just cometh from there.'

'What is 'appening there now?' she asked. 'Is my 'usband still stealing my clothes?'

'Your husband hath been taken to the Tower,' said Will.

'Ze Tower?' said a visibly shaken queen. 'Ze Bloody Tower?'

''Tis not the fault of the English that the bloody Tower is there,' said Will. 'It was a Frog who builteth it.'

'Non, *mon cheri*,' said the queen, smiling and showing her soot-blackened teeth. 'I mean is my 'usband in ze *Bloody* Tower where zose poor little princes were murdered and from where zey say nobody cometh out alive?'

Will shrugged his shoulders. 'All I knoweth,' he said, 'is that the king is under arrest for what hath been described as an act of infamy.'

'Ah, infamy, infamy,' said the queen, carrying on. 'Zey all 'ave it in for me.* What is to becometh of me now?'

'I suggesteth thou getteth back to Hampton Court immediately,' said Will, remembering her attempt to have her way with him on her last visit. 'Cromwell and Wolsey are plotting even now to taketh over the throne.'

'Thou art right, *mon cheri*,' said Marie. 'Zer are just two favours I wouldst asketh of zee before I rush away.'

Will bowed his head, dreading what was coming. 'Anything thou commandest, Your Majesty,' he said.

'I wouldst like zee to write in thy Royal Watcher column,' she said, 'zat I shouldst be instantly confirmed as ze one and only Queen of England, just in case my 'usband escapes from ze Bloody Tower and tries to pass himself off as ze queen.'

'Considereth it done,' said Will, knowing that nobody

Carry On film aficionados will recognise the 'infamy, infamy' line as one of the most famous penned for Kenneth Williams by scriptwriting master Talbot Rothwell.

had ever escaped from the Bloody Tower. 'And the other request?'

'Thou knowest thou driveth me crazy, William,' she said in a soft, husky voice, the sexual effect she was aiming for just slightly spoiled by the blackened teeth and the huge false wart that she had glued to the side of her nose. Even so, Will had to admit to a stirring in the breeches and he might have been tempted but for a sudden interruption.

'Oyez, oyez, oyez,' boomed from between the queen's legs as she sat on the bucket seat trying to entice Will by giving him teasing glimpses of the royal jewels.

'*Merde*!' said the queen. 'What is zat?'

'That is the town crier calling from downstairs,' said Will. 'He bringeth the latest tidings.'

'Hear ye,' came the voice between the queen's legs. 'Tis I Charles Dickhead with tidings for ye, Will. Can I cometh up?'

'I must not be seen here by a member of ze BBC,' said a suddenly anxious Queen Marie. 'Zey 'ave a news-sharing agreement with ze French Broadcasting Criers, and I doth not wish ze citizens of France to 'ear zat I am reduced to 'aving to look like an old 'ag. I shalt go down ze stairs as last time, pretending to be ze cleaning skivvy.'

She looked at Will and gave him the full black-teeth smile. 'But one day, William,' she promised, 'I will hath my way with zee and prove myself an old scrubber, *oui*?'

'*Oui*,' agreed Will, showing her to the stairs and then returning to the yellyphone.

116

'Thou can cometh up, Dickhead' he shouted. 'The door is openeth.'

'I admireth thy taste,' boomed Dickhead, as he settled on the bucket seat fighting for his breath.

'What doth thou mean?' said Will.

'That old skivvy I passeth on the stairs,' said Dickhead. 'She's just my sort. I'd loveth to giveth her one.'

'That,' said Will, 'was Henry's Queen Marie.'

Dickhead laughed. 'Pulleth the other one, Will,' he said. 'It hath got bells on it.'

'Thou hath heardst the news about the king?' said Will.

'Aye, 'tis why I am here,' said Dickhead. 'Hast thou any idea where he mighteth be now?'

'In the Tower, of course,' said Will. 'I thought thou knewest that.'

'Thou, Will, are behind with the tidings,' shouted Dickhead, for the whole of Tower Hamlets to hear. 'The king escaped his guards and runneth free. Methinks he didst bribe them.'

'With what?' said Will.

'He was wearing the queen's tiara at the time of his arrest, and an informant hath told the BBC that a captain of the guards was seen wearing it shortly after the king's escape.'

'I wonder where on earth he will turnest up next?' said Will.

No sooner were the words out of his mouth than a quiet voice came through Dickhead's legs on the bucket seat.

'Cooee, doth Will the Quill heareth me?'

Despite the faintness of the breathless-sounding voice, Will immediately recognised it as belonging to Queen Henrietta.

'Cometh thee up,' Will shouted between Dickhead's legs. 'The door is openeth.'

'Is it wise that we should be seen together?' said Dickhead. 'I doth not wishest to droppeth thee in it.'

'Don't worry,' said Will. 'I will introduce thee as a friend. It is good that thou art here to witness this. We shalt be able to produce a bumper issue of the *Times*.'

The king, still wearing Queen Marie's clothes, came staggering into the room exhausted after his run from the Tower - just half a mile away - and then the climb up the stairs.

He collapsed on to the bucket seat, which meant he was sitting on Dickhead's lap.

'I promise thee,' he said through gasping breaths, 'that heads are going to roll for this.'

It was the unmistakable voice of King Henry.

'What hath happened to Queen Henrietta?' asked Will.

'I proveth that I am the greatest actor in the whole of England,' said the king with a loud chuckle. 'As I layeth in my bed I hearest Wolsey and Cromwell plotting against me. I knewest I had to find a way out of Hampton Court otherwise they wouldst have held me prisoner there, and no doubt hath poisoned me by now. They were preparing me a dish of lampreys which accounted for the first of the Henrys.'*

'So thou art no longer Queen Henrietta?' said Will.

---

*King Henry I died after eating a dish of lampreys – eel-like fish with sucker mouths – in 1135.

118

'As if I would ever be anything but a man,' boomed Henry, then quickly getting off Dickhead's lap.

'Who doth this be?' Henry asked. 'Canst he be trusted, or shouldst I order his head to be cutteth off?'

'This is my good friend Charles Dickhead,' said Will. 'He is a tidings writer and crier with the BBC.'

'Thy good friend, eh?' said the king with a knowing look. 'He no doubteth responded to thy winking.'

'It's nothing like that,' said an aggrieved Will. 'We are just good friends.'

'Why art thy organisation so anti-king?' Henry asked Dickhead, not realising that he was talking to the man who was the most anti-Royal of all.

'We always tryeth to be balanced and impartial,' lied Dickhead.

'Then why doth thou giveth such extensive coverage to that mealy-mouthed wife of mine?' asked the king. 'She just hath to bat those large blue eyes of hers and she hath all the hacks eating out of her hand. Doth thou not realiseth that she tryeth to undermineth me, and thus the crown, with every sentence that she uttereth. Even worse than the BBC is that accursed *Panorama Times*. If ever I findeth out who publishes it and the identity of the Royal Watcher, I shalt personally carry out the execution with a blunt axe.'

''Tis good to know thy memory is now perfectly restored,' said Will, who was accustomed to hearing this sort of tirade from the king, while Dickhead was dwelling on the thought of what it would be like to be Nohead.

'What doth thou meanst?' said the king. 'I hath the

best memory in the whole of England.'

'But thou lost it,' said Will, 'or was that the work of a master actor as well?'

'I hath to admit that I hath no recollection of the last few days,' said the king. 'One minute I was supping a tankard of ale in the Peacock and Partridge, and the next I was lying in the Royal bed hearing Wolsey and Cromwell plotting to overthroweth me.'

'The Peacock and Partridge?' said Will, trying to keep the shock out of his voice. 'The inn at Windsor?'

'The very one,' said the king. 'They poureth the best ale in the whole of Surrey, and they hath a serving wench there who couldst knock thy eyes out with her jugs.'

Will churned inside with a mixture of anger, fear and jealousy. The king could only have been referring to Nell Grinn, the woman of his dreams who had promised herself to him once he was free of his sterile marriage. He knew he had to keep that fact to himself, because if ever the king discovered that he was the Royal Watcher it would implicate Nell, who was as innocent as a new-born babe (but much better built).

'What doth thou plan to doeth now?' asked Will. 'Why doth thou honoureth me with thy presence?'

Dickhead pulled a face behind the king's back and thumbed his nose.

'I wanteth thou to go to Hampton Court and fetcheth me my regal robes,' said Henry. 'I cannot commandeth respect whilst wearing the queen's clothes. Talketh only to the loyal Bernardo, and instructeth him to alert the Royal guard. Once I am dresseth as a king should be I shalt giveth the order to have Wolsey and Cromwell

120

arrested and thrown into the Tower.'

The king turned to Dickhead. 'Whilst thou art gone,' he said, 'I shalt sitteth here with thy good friend and adviseth him of what I expecteth of the BBC if they art to be allowed to continueth their broadcasts. He can telleth me the names of the tidings writers who hath been lambasting me, and I shalt hath their heads off. Then I shalt turn my attentions to my wife, and to the consideration of how I can getteth riddeth of her. I hath my eye on a serving wench who wouldst make me the perfect partner.'

Up on the roof, Claude de Bedsop noted what he had heard for Queen Marie's attention. Down in the garret, Will was trying to come to terms with the revelation that Henry had designs on his special girl. He secretly wished that King Henry would revert to being Queen Henrietta.

**Will the Winker
A portrait by
Hans Holbein**

Uneasy lies the head that wears a crown
which may belong to a King or a Queen.
Which is it to be? Henry or Henrietta?
Whether 'tis he or she, the future is
bright for his or her descendants,
For soothsayer Bernardo foresees the
striking of oil in the Windsor grounds.
So 'tis with relief, tempered with
regret over the conspiracy against
the King or Queen, that we can say,
'My friends, oil's well that ends well.'

122

8

THE cunning, conniving Cardinal Thomas Wolsey was trying on the king's crown for size when he was startled by the sight of a ghostwriter. He espied the stooping figure of Will the Quill tip-toeing along the Hampton Court corridor in quest of King Henry's clothes, and his suspicions were instantly aroused.

Wolsey leapt out in front of Will, making him jump so high that he invented the phrase, 'Thou scareth the shyte out of me.'

'Why art thou creeping by like a cat that hath just crepteth into the crypt, crapped and crepteth out again?' asked Wolsey accusingly. 'Thou hath mischief and deceit writ large upon thee.'

Will decided that flattery was the best form of defence. 'Why, Cardinal, that crown fitteth thee like a glove,' he said. ''Tis as if it were made for thee.'

Wolsey preened and pushed the crown tighter on to his huge head. 'Yea, it resteth easy 'pon my head,' he said, 'but thou hath not answered my question. Why art thou sneaking around as if thou hath something to hide?'

'Not I,' said Will. ''Tis just that I doth not wisheth to disturbeth thee whilst thy grace is obviously preparing for what wouldst be a most popular coronation.'

''Tis too early to talk of a crowning ceremony,' said Wolsey. 'The king remaineth on the loose, and not until we findeth him and returneth him to the Tower where he belongeth canst I layeth claim to the throne. Thou hath no idea at all where he mighteth be hiding?'

Will shrugged. 'Hath thou searched the homes for fallen women that he hath founded throughout London?' he said. 'Since he canst now qualifieth as a fallen queen, it wouldst maketh sense that he wouldst try to hideth out at one of the hostels.'

'Goodly thinking,' said Wolsey. 'I will sendeth guards to searcheth the homes forthwith.'

Lord Chancellor Thomas Cromwell came walking into the corridor. He was trying on one of the king's heavy gold chains bearing the Royal coat of arms. The enormous weight of it was forcing him to walk in a crouch.

Wolsey tried to remove the crown before Cromwell spotted it, but it had become stuck fast on his head.

'Art thou not being a little presumptive wearing the king's crown?' said Cromwell.

'And art thou not being equally presumptive wearing the king's finest chain?' said Wolsey.

'I doth weareth it for reasons of security,' said the Chancellor. 'There is no danger of anyone stealing it while it adorneth my neck.'

'Likewise with me,' said the Cardinal. 'Whilst I hath the king's crown on my head nobody wouldst dare tryeth to purloin it. I shalt looketh after it until we findeth a head that it fitteth.'

'Well it certainly doth not fit thine,' said Cromwell. 'Thou looketh like the court jester.'

'At least it hath not turned me into a hunchbacked dwarf as doth thy chain,' countered the Cardinal.

'Enough of this back biting,' said Cromwell. 'We

needeth to be united at this time of great crisis for our country and our monarchy. What news of the king's whereabouts?'

'I hath just this minute cometh up with an idea where he mighteth be hiding,' said Wolsey. 'I am about to order the guards to searcheth each of the king's homes for fallen women.'

'But they hath all been searched,' said Cromwell. ''Tis the first place I thoughteth of looking. I doth not think he hath left Tower Hamlets. His countenance is too well knowneth to be able to travel incognito. What thinkest thou, Will? Thou liveth in Tower Hamlets and knoweth the area well, doth thou not?'

'My view is that he wouldeth have gotteth as far away from the Tower as possible,' said Will. 'He is now probably disguised as an old peasant woman in the depths of Essex and being sheltered by a sympathetic Royalist.'

'I thinketh that will giveth us the right to claimeth the throne by default,' said Wolsey. 'We could putteth out a nationwide broadcast through the BBC, scripteth by Will here, that the king hath deserted his throne and his commitments to his countrymen. It would meaneth that he hath renounced his right to ruleth our great land and to all the privileges that go with it.'

'Yea, also that he hath deserted his wife,' said Cromwell. 'That wouldst turn public sympathy against him.'

'Nincompoop,' said Wolsey. 'That wouldst also turneth the public on the queen's side and they wouldst expecteth her to succeedeth to the throne.'

A minor point like that was easily brushed aside by the scheming Chancellor.

'We wouldst then put out another broadcast scripteth by Will,' he rationalised, 'in which we wouldst announceth, with greatest sorrow and sympathy, that the Queen grievest so much over her husband's desertion that she threwest herself out of the window. That wouldst make our citizens even more against Henry, and more responseth to a successor.'

'Thou art working well, Lord Chancellor,' said the Cardinal, wishing he had been first to have thought of such a devilish and devious plan. 'We wouldst giveth her a state funeral to appease her cousin King Francis, and inviteth all the royal dignitaries of Europe to attendeth and then stayeth for the coronation of the new King of England.'

'Long live Thomas of England,' the two conspirators announced together.

'Vivre Marie, the new Queen of England,' the eavesdropping Claude de Bedsop said quietly to himself from behind a corridor pot plant.

Will attempted to excuse himself from the sinister plot making. 'I must away,' he said. 'I hath urgent matters to attend.'

'Thou hath not yet explaineth thy presence here at my palace,' said the Cardinal.

Will was prepared for him. 'I hath cometh to collecteth my *Henry the Magnificent* book manuscript,' he said. 'I wouldst not wisheth anybody to findeth it and readeth how Henry sayeth in his very own words that he considereth himself the rightful king.'

126

'Thou thinkest most shrewdly,' said the Cardinal. 'Destroyeth the manuscript forthwith and writeth a new version in which King Henry wilt confesseth to all his manifold sins, including adultery, fornication, hypocrisy, gluttony...'

'Fraudulence,' added the Chancellor, 'thievery, deceit, avarice, treachery...'

'Forgery, embezzlement, intimidation, sodomy, pillage, rape,' listed the Cardinal. 'Debauchery, murder on a grand scale...'

'Bribery, corruption, depravity, immorality,' said the Chancellor. 'Covetousness, jealousy, idleness, felony, extortion, wife-beating...'

Claude the Fraud made a note to report that to King Francis.

'Wench chasing,' was the one contribution from Will, his eye going on the blink as he remembered that the king had been trying to have his royal way with Nell Grinn.

'Blasphemy, desecration, grave robbing, bestiality,' continued the Cardinal. 'Singing out of tune and ruining choir practice...'

'Methinks I hath enough to be going on with,' said Will, startled that they had in a way stumbled on his master plan.

He had already drawn up confessions, not only for the king but also for Wolsey and Cromwell that, at a time to suit Dickhead's republican movement, would be broadcast by town criers across the land. This would not only bring down the king, but Wolsey and Cromwell along with him.

127

He pretended to go off in search of the manuscript, and looked instead for Bernardo.

The king's loyal right-hand man was leaking tears, both from his good eye and the false one, when Will eventually located him hiding in an apple tree in the orchard where he had first started working at Hampton Court. Will was taken to him by the footman that he had met doing amazing things with a maid in the maze, and who had been instructed by Bernardo to lead him to the orchard if he arrived at the Court.

'Those evil traitors hath locked my king in the Tower,' he sobbed. 'I hideth here because I knoweth they wilt maketh me a prisoner next.'

Bernardo's glass eye radiated sunshine when Will told him the tidings about the king's presence at his garret.

'He needeth his Royal robes,' said Will, 'and for you to alert the Royal guard, but thou must maketh sure that the Cardinal and Lord Chancellor knoweth nothing of what lies afoot.'

'I will taketh thee to the king's room by a secret back passage,' said Bernardo. 'Thou canst taketh his clothes while I maketh contact with the guards. They remaineth loyal to the king. The captain is a good and dependable royalist who hath often been up the king's back passage.'

Will followed Bernado into the secret entrance and they crept along a winding corridor until coming to a sliding door that led into the king's bedroom.

'This is what the king's staff knoweth as the Maid's Entrance,' said Bernardo, winking with his good eye.

'He doth often summon them for a private audience. I hath seen in my crystal eye that one day they wilt hath a merry stage play about it called, *An Audience with King Henry.*'

Hans Holbein, painting the king's bedroom ceiling, nearly fell off his ladder with shock as a concealed door in the oak-panelling slid open and Bernardo and Will came through.

'Vas is going up?' he said. 'Thou nearly maketh me hit zer ceiling.'

''Tis all right,' Bernardo said to Will. 'Hans is a loyal friend to the king. We art all united in our hatred of Wolsey and Cromwell.'

'Zey hath ordered me to paint over zer looking glasses zat ze king hef in zer ceiling,' said Hans. 'Zey art gross spoilsports. Ven I hef finished zer painting over, I hef to go and paint zer face of zer Cardinal on top of all zer portraits of zer king.'

'Doth Cromwell knoweth this?' asked Bernardo.

Hans shrugged. 'Zis I do not know,' he said. 'I hef my orders from zer Cardinal. All I hef been told by zer Chancellor is zat I must paint his face over every portrait of zer Queen zat ve hef in Hampton Court.'

'That must be irksome for thee painting over your original work,' said Will.

'I can hardly face it,' said Hans.

'Thou shouldst not paint too quickly, Hans,' advised Bernardo. 'I needst not looketh in my crystal eye to telleth that the king will be backeth on the throne before the sun setteth.'

Will had just selected the king's robes, a crown and

a gold chain when there was a commotion outside the door.

Hans, who could see over the top of the door from his ladder, warned, 'It is zer Cardinal's guards, and zey comst zis vay.'

'Quick,' said Bernardo, 'into the secret passage.'

He bundled Will through the sliding door, and pointed along the corridor. 'You goeth that way,' he said. 'I must goeth the opposite way to tippeth off the Royal guard. Telleth the king that we wilt rendezvous in the same place where we metteth in the orchard at eight of the clock.'

Will raced blindly along the twisting and turning corridor, handicapped by the weight of the king's apparel. He decided that to make his progress easier it would make sense to put on the robes. He hung the gold chain around his neck and placed the crown on his head. Now he was able to move more freely, and he soon left the sound of the Cardinal's guards behind him after hearing them asking Hans if he had seen Bernardo.

'For zer life of me, I cannot picture vat he looks like,' said the loyal Hans.

He had run all of a quarter mile along darkened passages before coming to a sliding door identical to the one that had led into the king's bedroom. Will slid it open and found himself looking straight into the face of Queen Marie, who gave a shriek of fright.

'Your 'ighness,' she said, giving a double take. 'But thou art not your 'ighness.'

Will's right eye was blinking at maximum speed.

'Why art thou wearing ze king's clothes?' Marie

asked. 'And 'is crown and Royal chain. 'e will crown zee and pull thy chain if 'e finds out zat thou art taking over ze throne.'

'I weareth them for the king,' said a flustered Will, wondering how much he could tell Henry's wife.

'Claude 'as told me zat 'Enri is 'oled up in thy 'ome' said Marie, wrapping her fourteen fingers around Will's hands and leading him to her four-poster bed. She patted the side of the bed to indicate that he should sit alongside her.

'Ze crown and ze chain zey suit zee, *mon cheri*,' she said. 'I wouldst much rather thou were my king zan zat 'orrid 'Enri. Claude tells me zat he wishes to get rid of me so zat 'e can 'ave a serving wench in my place. I asketh thou! A serving wench as ze Queen of England. 'Enri 'as clearly lost 'is *billes*, or as ze English wouldst say, marbles.'

Will was now driven by selfish motives. 'Thou doth not want him to marry the serving wench and neither doth I,' he said.

'Why, Will,' said Marie, 'I 'ave ze suspicion zat zere is *l'amour* involved 'ere. Doth thou knowest zis serving wench? Is she worthy of ze crown of England? Is she more beautiful zan me?'

'Methinks she is just not right for ze throne,' said Will, lying through his teeth because in his eyes she was like a princess.

'But 'ow can I stop 'Enri making a fool of 'imself and marrying zis girl at my expense?' said Marie. 'I wouldst not admit zis to anybody else, Will, but I am deeply in love wiz 'Enri, as badly as 'e 'as treated me. I enjoy

131

being ze Queen of England and I am proud of being 'is wife. Now 'e doth wanteth to cast me aside for a wench who serveth ale. My 'eart and my pride 'urteth so much I couldst die.'

Henry, Will knew, would give her that privilege if he could. It was only the prospect of being invaded by King Francis and his mighty army that had stopped him from chopping off her head long ago.

Will fumbled inside his breeches and pulled out a sheet of parchment that he had prepared days before. This was the confession that he had forged in the king's name and which Charles Dickhead was going to broadcast from the Greenwich town hall steps with the objective of starting a revolution that would lead to England becoming a republic. It read:

I Henry VIII doth solemnly confess in the hearing of the witnesses here present that I hath been guilty of treachery, adultery, debauchery, corruption and murder most foul. I am not worthy any longer to holdeth the honour of King of England, and I hereby abdicate the throne so that our great country can becometh united as a Republic without any more Royal taxes or executions at a king's whim. I asketh thy understanding and the forgiveness of the Almighty for all my sins commited in the name of the King of England, and I prayeth that thou will spare me my life so that I canneth liveth out my days in a nice warm cell in the Tower of London.

Will handed the confession to Marie. She read it in stunned silence.

'*Mon Dieu*, zis is 'Enri's signature,' she said, studying the scrawl at the bottom of the parchment.

'A clever forgery,' said Will. 'Yet it can saveth thy marriage.'

'But 'ow?' said Marie. ''Enri would never let zis be read aloud in public.'

'I was ready to have it broadcast by the BBC,' said Will. 'But methinks it will be better in thy possession. Shouldst he threaten that he is divorcing thee so that he can marryeth the serving wench, tell him that thou wilt releaseth this confession to the *Times*.'

''e wouldst chop off my 'ead,' said Marie.

'Not whilst thy cousin is King of France,' said Will. 'Thy husband, along with Wolsey and Cromwell, hath dug so deep into the nation's coffers for their own selfish needs that they hath allowed England's army to runneth down. We hath neither the arms nor the men to beat off a French invasion. The spirit of Agincourt hath long since withered and died on the altar of King Henry's greed.'

'But what about thy dream of England becoming a Republic?' said Marie.

''Tis a dream that wilt never be fulfilled,' admitted Will sadly. 'The Royal publicity machine hath worked too smoothly. The English will always want a monarchy, and seemeth almost to enjoyeth being ruled by parasites. There wilt never be a Republic in this country.'

'Neither in France,' said Marie. 'The citizens doth not 'ave ze appetite for revolution.'

She patted Will on the crown. ''Tis a noble zing zat thou doest,' the Queen said. 'Ze piece of paper zat I holdeth in my 'and meaneth piss in our time. My cousin will not invade England while I am married to 'Enri. But I cannot help zinking zat zere is somzing deeper 'ere, zat it involves ze serving wench and zat thou 'ath let your 'eart rule thy 'ead.'

'Thou art a very perceptive lady, thy Majesty,' said Will. ''Tis true that I hath losteth my heart to the wench. But the main reason for my decision not to releaseth the confession publicly is that my partner, Charles Dickhead, is too good a man for me to alloweth him to give Henry an excuse to cutteth off his head. I hath already losteth the much-loved head of my father to his axe. Charles hath been like a second father to me, and he is the one who wouldst be putting his head on the block by reading out the confession. He wouldst be thrown into the Tower and executed before the cock croweth the next morning.'

'So 'ow wilt thou explaineth all zis to thy ami, Monsieur Dick'ead?'

'I shalt telleth him to be satisfied with producing the alternative voice of the public with his laudable magazine, the *Panorama Times*,' said Will. 'We can continueth being a thorn prick in the king's side...'

'A what prick iz zis?'

'A thorn prick,' repeated Will.

'Ah, you English, you are always so prick conscious.'

'We shalt just hath to be patient and wait for the Royals to buryeth themselves,' said Will. 'I am sureth that one day they wilt hath a divorce too many, and the citizens of England wilt say "enough is enough".'

Marie was just about to make a grab for Will's hidden jewels when the Cardinal's guards hammered on her bedroom door. 'Open up in the esteemed name of Cardinal Wolsey,' came the command. 'Art thou hiding Bernardo in there?'

'No way!' shouted Marie, buying time. 'I don't like zat man 'aving his eye on me.'

'*Vîte*,' she said to Will, 'getteth zose clothes to ze king so zat he can regaineth control from ze wicked Cardinal and Chancellor.'

'Wilt thou be all right?' asked Will, making for the secret door.

'*Oui, mon cheri,*' said Marie. 'Zey dare not toucheth me. I am ze undisputed Queen of England now zat zere is no 'Enriette to challenge me.'

Will dashed off back to Tower Hamlets, carrying the king's robe and the crown and the chain in an old sack that he had found in the Hampton Court garden.

He was finding it hard to believe that here he was, the Royal Watcher, taking his life in his hands trying to get the king restored to the throne.

Was he doing it for the life of Charles Dickhead or the love of Nell Grinn? Will felt it was for a bit of both... and certainly for a bit of the other.

**Will the Winker
A portrait by
Hans Holbein**

God save the King! That these words
should tumble from my lips
Leaves me with a reeling mind.
What will the morrow bring after today's
mirth and madness?
Can it be true that I am on the King's
side in the power struggle?
Verily, it is the promise of a wench's
hand and sweet lips
That hath turned my head, but surely not
enough to warrant a change of heart.

9

WILL was astonished to hear singing voices coming from the downstairs yellyphone when he arrived back at the front door of the rectory carrying the king's clothes, crown and chain. Before leaving for Hampton Court they had agreed on using 'Greensleeves' as the password to avoid any unwelcome callers making their way up to the garret.

'Hello,' he shouted into the bucket. 'Greensleeves.'

There was a lull in the singing. 'We doth not doeth requests,' came back the clearly slurred voice of King Henry.

'Greensleeves,' repeated Will, louder.

'All right, if thou insist,' said the king.

There were suddenly three voices sounding in Will's ear. They were singing 'Greensleeves', and he had to admit that the harmony was not half bad. He could hear that the king's strong baritone was the lead voice, Charles Dickhead was, unmistakeably, providing a booming bass. His oyez-oyez-oyez at the end of each line added a catchy rhythmical touch. But who on earth was that singing alto?

Will pushed at the front door. It was open, and he went up the twelve narrow flights of stairs with some trepidation. He arrived, breathless, at the garret to discover it crowded with the king, Dickhead and a plainly inebriated Reverend Neil Downer.

Squeezing into a room that was virtually full when

occupied by one person, Will found a party atmosphere. The king was sitting on Dickhead's lap on the bucket seat, and the Reverend Downer was leaning against Will's desk. Each of them had half-empty bottles of mead in their hands.

'Do forgiveth me, my son,' said a beaming Reverend Downer. 'I beheld the king making his way up the stairs to thy room, and I thought it my duty to make him feeleth at home in thy absence. So I just popped up with a few bottles of mead.'

'And an excellent and potent brew it is, too,' said the king, who had four empty bottles at his feet as evidence that he had drunk twice as much as the other two. 'Your good friend Dickhead here is now my good friend also, and the Reverend Downer is such a lovely man that I am considering making him the next Cardinal.'

'And I,' announced a positively glowing Dickhead, 'am to be the king's new public relations officer at a salary of fifty-two crowns a year. At last I can goeth and telleth the BBC to stuffeth themselves. No more oyez-oyez-oyezing for me. From now on my voice is that of the king's.'

Will tried hard not to gape.

'The king hath promised me a bonus of one hundred golden crowns if I can getteth the *Panorama Times* shutteth down,' Dickhead added. 'For two hundred golden crowns, I hath told him that I will seize it and turn it into a Royalist magazine with the motto, "Hurrah for Henry."'

'And what about that blaggard, the Royal Watcher?' said the king. 'I hath promised thee three hundred gold coins for his identity.'

Dickhead winked at Will, whose right eye winked back ten fold. 'I will see that he is silenced,' he said. 'But even one thousand coins will not buyeth his identity. He hath guarded it so well that nobody knoweth whom he is.'

So every man, thought Will, hath his price. Here was Dickhead selling his soul for fifty-two crowns a year, plus bonuses, and he himself had come over to the king's side for the hand of Nell Grinn.

'Well, what news doth thou bringeth?' asked the king, the bottle of mead to his mouth.

Will took the robes, crown and chain from the sack and placed them on the desk. 'Wolsey and Cromwell art contesting with each other as to who shouldst be the next king,' he reported. 'They art wiping out all evidence of your existence, even down to painting thy face off thy portraits.'

'The dirtieth rotten scoundrels,' said the king. 'Their heads wilt roll before nightfall.'

The Reverend Downer put up a hand, and made a sign of the cross. 'But thy Majesty, thou hath promised me on thy oath that thou wilt stop all the blood-letting,' he said. 'If I am to become Cardinal I wouldst first of all abolish capital punishment.'

'Just two more heads,' said Henry, 'then thou canst hath thy way. Thy first job as Cardinal will be to overseeth my divorce and then my marriage to the serving wench.'

Will felt a chill like a knife blade to his heart.

Reverend Downer put up a hand, and made another

sign of the cross. 'But thy Majesty, thou hath promised me on thy oath that thou wilt stay true to thy marriage vows,' he said. 'If I am to become Cardinal I wouldst second of all abolish divorce.'

'Just one more marriage,' said Henry, 'then thou canst hath thy way.' Quietly he thought to himself that perhaps he had been a little hasty to have offered Downer the role of Cardinal. He would change the appointment to Bishop of Cumberland. That seemed far enough away for a man who wished to restricteth him so.

The king took off Queen Marie's dress and put on his robe, and then his crown and chain. The transformation was such that both Downer and Dickhead dropped to one knee as a sign of allegiance. 'Proof,' thought Will, 'that clothes maketh the man.'

King Henry had supped enough mead to have knocked over a horse, but his boast that he was 'the greatest drinker in the whole of England' truly held water.

'Bringeth my charger,' he roared. 'We are off to war!'

All the local blacksmith could supply was two mules, on which the king and Will headed for Hampton Court and a showdown with Wolsey and Cromwell.

Henry felt the occasion leant itself to the cry of one of his predecessors on the English throne. 'God for Harry!' he roared. 'England and Saint George!'*

The only response the king got was a window of a nearby house flying open and an old, bad-tempered

*From Shakespeare's *Henry V* before the Battle of Agincourt:
I see you stand like greyhounds in the slips,
Straining upon the start. The game's afoot:
Follow your spirit; and upon this charge
Cry 'God for Harry! England and Saint George!'

crow throwing her pail of waste over him.

'Ee-aw!' bellowed Henry's mule.

And they set off for battle.

It was just after eight of the clock when the still drunk king and Will arrived at their rendezvous in the orchard. Bernardo was there alone.

'Where art my loyal and brave guards?' asked the king. 'They art hidden in the trees?'

Bernardo looked fearful and embarrassed. Even his false eye was frightened to look at the king. 'There art no guards,' he said.

'No guards?' roared the king. 'But how art I to fight for my throne without guards? 'Tis like king Arthur going into his day without his knights.'

'They are on strike, my liege,' Bernardo said, almost in a whisper.

'On strike?' said an apoplectic and suddenly sobering Henry. 'What doth thou mean, on strike?'

'They hath not been paid these past six months,' said Bernardo. 'Wolsey hath been using their money to payeth the builders of his latest palace. The guards sayeth they will no longer slay without pay.'

'Heads will roll for this,' promised Henry.

Bernardo shook his head. 'I art afraid not, thy Majesty,' he said. 'The executioners hath laid down their axes. They too hath not been paid. They sayeth they will no longer choppeth unless they coppeth.'

'Well go and findeth me some good olde yeomen of England,' ordered the king. 'Farmers with arms like English oak firing arrows good and true wilt helpeth

141

me rid myself of the traitors Wolsey and Cromwell.'

Another shake of the head from Bernardo. 'I hath already tried to persuadeth them to join thee in thy moment of need, my liege,' he said. 'But they are that vexed over the taxes they hath to pay that they sayeth their fire is no longer for hire.'

'So it is left to we few, we happy few, we band of brothers,' he said, looking at Bernardo and the less than enthusiastic Will, 'who must end this revolt by Wolsey and Cromwell.'

'I feel it my duty to report, sire,' said Bernardo, 'that the Cardinal and the Lord Chancellor are protected by two hundred well-paid guards, who art armed to the very teeth and on a golden-ball bonus to present either of thy testicles to them.'

'So what doth I do?' said a despairing king.

'I hath an idea,' said the inventive Will the Quill.

'A bag of gold if it regaineth my throne,' said the king.

'Doth we accepteth that we cannot match their armoury?' asked Will.

'That goeth without saying, even though I am the greatest swordsman in the whole of England,' said Henry.

'Then we must overcome them with stealth,' said Will. 'Agreed?'

Henry and Bernardo nodded.

'Well I hath been working on an idea with just such an eventuality as this in mind,' said Will. 'We will needeth to return to my abode so that I can showest it to thee.'

'Ordereth the grooms to saddle us up three trusty

142

steeds,' said the king.

Bernardo went back into the head shaking routine. 'Canst be done, thy Majesty,' he said. 'The stable workers art on strike because they too hath not been paid. They sayeth no groats, no oats.'

"Tis not any of my doing,' said an aggrieved Henry. 'I left matters of the treasury to Wolsey and Cromwell, while I concentrateth on such vital matters as hunting, fishing, jousting, real tennis, singing, composing, playing the virginals, wooing, marrying, divorcing, wooing and marrying again, divorcing, wooing, marrying, drinking and eating. God, England hath never had such an industrious king and this is the way that I am payeth back. Heads will roll.'

Bernardo shook his head.

'Wrists will be slapped then,' vowed Henry as he climbed back on to his mule and headed for Tower Hamlets.

Bernardo rode on Will's mule, and Will scooted along at twice their speed on small, hard, rounded apples attached to his shoes. He called them Granny Smith's roller skoots.

It was after midnight and the crypt of St Paul's church, Tower Hamlets, was, to put it mildly, a creepy place to be. Will needed this setting to show off his concept. The king and Bernardo stayed outside the crypt door with the Reverend Neil Downer, who was holding a lantern. 'Giveth me ten minutes, and then thou mayst follow me in,' said Will as he disappeared behind the door leading to where the church vaults housed tombs of long-dead and gone priests and leading parishioners.

Reverend Downer had doused the light in the lantern by the time he showed the king and Bernardo into the crypt. It was pitch black inside, and Henry quietly cussed as he bumped into a tomb.

'Standeth still and just watcheth,' called a muffled voice in hollow tones that reverberated around the crypt.

Suddenly the king let out a piercing scream as, rising before his eyes and lit bright, came the disembodied head of Anne Boleyn, his second wife whom he had executed for her alleged adultery and witchcraft. Then, ten feet away, followed the head of his fifth wife Catherine Howard, who also fell under Henry's axe for adultery.

'Wilt thou, Henry VIII of England,' inquired the eerie, hollow voice, 'repent ye of all thy sins and transgressions, and confess to the Almighty that thou hath erred in thy ways? And wilt thou vow in future to serve thy country unselfishly and, at all times, observing the needs of others?'

Henry dropped on his knees, banging his head against the tomb. 'I doth repent a thousand fold, My Lord,' he said, 'and I vow to do all that thou asketh of me. I beggeth the forgiveness of my two wives here for being so hasty to the axe, and vow not to chop off the heads of any more of my wives.'

The muffled voice was just about to get him to promise to leave serving wenches be when a third head appeared. This was under the arm of a walking, headless corpse.

King Henry and Bernardo could take no more. They raced out of the crypt, colliding with each other and

144

tombstones as things went bump in the night. Will was already outside, looking as frightened as they.

Reverend Downer, who had relit the lantern, joined them at a casual gait.

'I am being haunted by the two wives that I beheaded,' said the king. 'I meant them no harm. What I said was "next please" and the executioner thought I said "necks please".'

A likely story, thought Will. ''Tis nothing to worry thyself about,' he said. 'That was my work.'

'What was thy work?' said the still quaking king.

'The heads,' said Will. 'They were pig bladders. I filleth them with air and placeth them on the end of thin poles.'

'But the bright faces,' said Henry. 'They were without question the complete likeness of my two dear, sweet departed wives.'

'They were painteth for me by Hans Holbein,' explained Will. 'He useth a newly discovered luminous paint that shineth in the dark.'

'And the voice?' said the king. 'Art thou going to tell me that was not the Almighty I was confessing to?'

'That was my voice relayed through one of my yellyphone buckets,' admitted Will.

'But what thou were saying was treasonable,' seethed Henry.

'I needeth to maketh it as real as possible,' said Will. 'How doth thou think Wolsey and Cromwell will react if, in the middle of the night, they seeth thy disembodied head rising above their bed?'

'But one small point seemeth to hath escapeth thy

145

attention,' said the king. 'I am very much aliveth and intendeth to be for some years yet.'

'Our good friend Dickhead can put out a BBC broadcast that thou art believeth to hath drowned trying to escapeth Wolsey's guards,' said Will. 'Then thou wilt suddenly appeareth like a vision from hell in the bedrooms of both Wolsey and Cromwell. I wilt script thee the words to sayeth that will frighten them into giving up any notion of replacing thee on the throne.'

'I hath one question,' said Bernardo, who was still shaking from his experience in the crypt and, indeed, his false eye was still wide with shock. 'Who was the third person that thou introduced to the little playlet?'

Will was seen to shrug in the flickering shadows thrown out by the lantern. 'That I knoweth not,' he said. 'It is why I myself ranneth out of the crypt as fast as my legs wouldst carryeth me.'

'You mean he was a *real* ghost?' said the king.

Will nodded. 'He was certainly not one of my making,' he said. 'I hath yet to perfect the moving body effect.'

Reverend Downer put the lantern up to his face and a finger to his lips. 'We shouldst not talk too loudly about the third apparition,' he said. 'He is on the conscience of us all here in Tower Hamlets. Twenty or so years ago the local grave digger said that he wished to be buried in the crypt at St Paul's. He was takeneth too literally by an over-enthusiastic curate. He instantly granted him his wish, but forgotteth to wait for him to first of all expire. The grave digger was buried alive in one of his own graves, and he has been walking the area ever since trying to get support for the theory that his death was not accidental but murder most foul. The fact that the curate later married the grave digger's widow certainly caused a few eyebrows to be raiseth.'

As they stood listening to Downer's ghost story, a black cat crept into the crypt, crapped and crept out again.

Henry sniffed the cold night air outside the crypt. 'The ghost of the grave digger,' he said, 'doth certainly kick up a stink.'

They returned to the rectory where the Reverend Downer gave up his bed for the king and Bernardo. Luckily, it was a king-size bed.

Will retired to his garret to plan the haunting of Hampton Court, reflecting on the fact that he had originally thought up the ghost heads idea to frighten the life out of King Henry. He felt that in many ways he had achieved that aim. In fact the king became the first Royal to use the time-honoured phrase, 'Thou scareth the shyte out of me.'

He found dear old Charles Dickhead on the garret room floor just coming out of a heavy, mead-induced sleep.

'We wanteth thee to get out a BBC broadcast tomorrow that the king is dead,' Will said.

'The king is dead!' said a suddenly sorrowful Dickhead. 'Two days ago I would hath rejoiceth, but having met the man I foundeth that I really liked him. He was, taking him warts 'n' all, a fitting person to weareth the English crown, and I was looking forward to pocketing his gold.'

'The king is *not* dead,' said Will.

'Hurrah,' said the still dozy, hungover Dickhead. 'The king is alive. Long live the king. And long live my job as his PR officer.'

'We wanteth to lure Wolsey and Cromwell into thinking he is dead,' said Will. 'Thou canst put out an all-points bulletin through the network of BBC criers tomorrow announcing that the king is believed to have drowneth in the River Thames near the Tower when trying to escapeth from Wolsey's guards. Give it a nice conspiratorial spin, so that the public turneth against Wolsey and Cromwell. Then there will be no sympathy or support for them when they are thrown into the Tower.'

'What of the Royal Watcher now?' asked Dickhead. 'Art thou disgusted with the way that I hath sold myself for the king's coin?'

'I would doeth the same in thy position,' admitted Will. 'But it will not need the *Panorama Times* nor the Royal Watcher to get rid of the monarchy. The Royals will eventually dig their own graves by their contemptuous behaviour.'

Will lay down to sleep, and as his mind wandered on the events of the day he spoke aloud. 'The Royal Watcher is sheathing his venomous quill,' he said. 'One day somebody will write that the pen is mightier than the sword.' This much is true, and it will be the pen rather than the sword that finally finishes off the monarchy. The king hath won on this occasion, but I

'Playwright and novelist Edward George Bulwer-Lytton (Baron Lytton) penned this line for his play, *Richelieu* (1838): 'Beneath the rule of men entirely great... The pen is mightier than the sword.'

may yet hath a personal score to settle with our Henry. This is not so much to do with pens, as penises.'

There was quiet lunchtime trade at the Peacock and Partridge when Will called in for a quick chat with Nell. She looked more beautiful than ever to his eyes and she made his heart swell when she blew him a kiss from across the bar room.

Lemmie Pulham, the landlord, was less pleased to see Will. He did not approve of him as a proper suitor for his adopted daughter.

Pulham recalled the note attached to her foot when she was left on their doorstep, 'One day she will bring thee riches beyond thy dreams.'

Well, Will the Quill was hardly likely to be the man to achieve this. He was penniless to the point where they sayeth of him, 'he doth not hath a pot to piss in.' King Henry, on the other hand, had secretly offered Pulham a payment of two hundred gold coins for his adopted daughter's hand in marriage once the minor matter of getting rid of his present queen was sorted out. That would set Pulham up for his old age, and he would be able to sit on the other side of the bar and let the wenches with the boiling over dumplings wait on him for a change.

Will waited for Nell to join him in the quietest corner of the bar. He was quite prosperous for a change, having been paid one crown by Claude de Bedsop for his interview with Queen Marie in the *Times*. The fee had been dropped by four crowns because of the unfortunate mix up when the queen had mentioned

Henry's affairs with *filles* and he had thought she had said fillies. It would, thought Will, have made the story much less compelling because everybody knew that the king was always chasing after girls. In newspaper speak, it was 'king goes with horse, story; king goes with girl, so what?'

Pulham poured him a tankard of best ale, and was pleasantly surprised, nay astonished, to be handed a gold coin rather than being asked to 'putteth it on the slate'. He bit the coin just to check that it was genuine. There had been a lot of forgers at work lately, and he had needed to make Nell pay more heed after she had accepted shirt buttons for a round of drinks.

Will had everything in place for that night's haunting visit to Hampton Court. The BBC town criers would be spreading news of the king's presumed death by drowning in the teatime bulletins, and Dickhead made certain that the chief Thames-side crier shouted the news within hearing of Hampton Court. The script he prepared for the criers showed his new standing as one of the king's men. It read:

Oyez, oyez, oyez. Five O'clock and all's not well. Hear ye that His Majesty King Henry VIII, King of all England, Defender of the Faith, Henry the Magnificent, and an all-round good egg, hath this day been reported 'missing believed drowned'. He was criminally chased into the River Thames by ruffian guards under the command of Cardinal Wolsey. The reign of our great king started in the year of our Lord 1509, and the thirty years he hath been on the throne hath been the most prosperous in England's long and proud history. His Majesty, the finest sportsman, musician, composer, jouster and hunter in the whole of England, was such a generous soul that he gaveth too much power and control to Wolsey and his henchman Thomas Cromwell, the Lord Chancellor. Now they hath done for him, and we waiteth to see whether either one of them will attempt to take over the throne at a time when true Englishmen are mourning the loss of their greatest monarch. King Henry leaves a widow, Queen Marie, who will be best off returning home to France for all the chance she hath of staying on the throne. Listen tomorrow for more exclusive news on this Royal sensation. This bulletin has been brought to thee by the brewers of Thames Mead, that many thinketh is the finest drink thou ever could drinketh. Don't just thinketh. Drinketh.

The sentence about Queen Marie had been added at the king's insistence. He was hoping that she would believe that he had drowned and sneak off home to France, which would leave him clear to divorce her for desertion.

They had had a few problems with the king that morning at the rectory. He had one of his barking fits, but the Reverend Downer quickly solved the problem by taking him for a walk across Tower Green. The king was fine once he had relieved himself against a tree.

Bernardo rode back to Hampton Court and told

Hans Holbein the plan, and he painted an exact likeness of the king's face on to a pig bladder in luminous paint. Henry had complained that it made him look as fat as a pig, and Will agreed not to blow the bladder up to its full extent so that the king's face looked a little less plump.

Nell joined Will once Pulham had gone into the back courtyard to supervise the delivery of barrels of ale. 'Hello, stranger,' she said, stealing a kiss out of sight of the other customers. 'I wondered if I would ever see thee again.'

'I've been up to mine eyes with the History of England book,' he said. 'I wanteth to hath it finished so that I can get enough money from a publisher to payeth for my divorce and leaveth myself free to marry thee.'

Will looked hard into her eyes. 'Thou art still promised to me?' he said, feeling an unusual tension.

'I always shalt be,' she said. 'But thou must not talketh about it here in the inn. My father doth not liketh us seeing each other.'

'It's the king, I knoweth it is,' said Will.

'What doth thou mean?' said Nell.

'I knoweth that the king hath been seeing you.'

'But not from my choosing. He cometh as a customer, and maketh a nuisance of himself.'

'Hath he proposed marriage?'

'Goodness, how could he when he hath a wife already?' said Nell, and then suddenly averting her gaze.

'Why doth thou looketh away?' Will asked.

'Because I am here to heareth all that thou sayeth,' said Pulham, who had arrived back without Will realising it. 'I warneth thee now, stay away from my daughter.'

'But we loveth each other.'

'It's true, father,' said Nell.

'Cockybull clacklebum!' exclaimed Pulham in his country manner. 'Love doth not payeth the bills.'

Pulham glared at Will. 'And thou canst stop winking,' he said. 'Thou will not getteth around me that way.'

'It was Will's winking that first attracteth me to him, father.'

'Well I thinketh that he hath a blinking cheek,' said Pulham.

'But I wanteth your daughter's hand in marriage, sire,' said Will, wondering whether his cheek had developed a tick as well as his eye.

'Not even a finger wilt thou get,' said Pulham. 'What canst thou offer her compared with the King of England?'

Will thought for a moment, hoping desperately that his writer's brain would come up with an answer. The king had Hampton Court and six other palaces, while he had a rented garret in which you could not swing a kilt; the king had a bottomless purse including all the tax money that he required, while he had less than one gold coin; the king had servants waiting at his beck and call, while he had to wait on himself.

'What I hath to offer, sire, money could not buy,' he said finally. 'I wouldst give her love and happiness. That is something that the king hath never been able to give any of his many wives.'

'Be that as it may,' said Pulham, 'I doth not want thee seeing my daughter again. I would now asketh thee to leave the premises.'

Will walked out of the Peacock and Partridge with heavy tread and heavy heart.

Behind him, Nell was crying into the beer that she was serving to customers. They later commented that it was the strongest they had known their ale to taste.

Will silently pledged to return for Nell's hand, but now he had to give all his concentration to restoring to the English throne his biggest rival for her love. He still had hope because Queen Marie was not going to let Henry go without a fight, and now she had his 'confession' with which to blackmail him into staying with her.

The next twenty-four hours, thought Will, would one day be writ large in his history book.

The king, meantime, was being prepared for the journey to Hampton Court. He could not travel as himself because by the time he started out the news would have been broadcast of his presumed death by drowning.

It was the idea of the Reverend Neil Downer that he should make the journey in a coffin as a dead man. 'Who is going to think that the King of England is being carried along in a coffin?' he said. 'To Keep any snooper away we can paint a white cross on the coffin lid so that people will thinketh that the dead person died of the plague. Nobody will want to go near it.'

'Including me,' said Bernardo. 'Not if he's got the plague.'

''Tis only make-believe,' said the Reverend Downer,

who was still hoping to land the job of Cardinal.

His was quite a bright idea. What was no so bright was to start the 'dead man's' final journey from the garret. Bernardo and Dickhead were under severe strain from the weight of the coffin as they struggled with it down the twelve flights of stairs, and it was not until they were two-thirds of the way down that Reverend Downer suggested that perhaps it might have been wiser to have started from the first floor.

At one stage they stumbled with it and the coffin titled to such an angle that the king sat up with the lid balanced on his head. It frightened the living daylights out of Mrs Malrooney, the *real* cleaning skivvy, who was coming up the stairs to scrub the rectory floor.

Once down in the street, they placed the coffin on a cart being pulled by the two mules and set off for Hampton Court.

Inside the coffin, Henry could be heard shouting, 'God for Harry! England and Saint George!'

**Will the Winker
A portrait by
Hans Holbein**

Tis as a make-believe ghost that Henry
next enters Hampton Court,
But how many real ghosts hath he set
on a haunting path,
Minus head and without pattern of life
nor feeling for day or night?
What true spirits and spectres will be
awakened when they know he is afoot?
It could yet be that the King of England
hath saved his life,
But, wait, hath he saved his soul?

10

IT was just past three o'clock of the morning when the small haunting party gathered in the Hampton Court orchard. Will carried Henry's luminous ghost head, mounted on a pole and covered by cloth. The king held the yellyphone bucket, through which he was to make his demands of Wolsey and Cromwell. They were an hour later than intended. The king had to learn his scripted lines because it was pointed out by Dickhead that he would not be able to see to read in the darkened corridor.

Bernardo led the way to the secret back passage, and it was agreed that Wolsey would be the first target. His bedroom was on the north side of the west wing. 'Whatever thou doeth,' Will said to the king, 'do not starteth on thy script until we knoweth for sure that Wolsey is awaketh.'

'How will I knoweth from outside the room?' Henry asked.

'Believeth me,' said Will, 'thou shalt heareth his shriek. Thou wilt then need to talk rapidly before the guards outside the bedroom door burst in, by which time both the ghost head and I will be back in the secret passage with thee. My calculation is that we will hath just one minute to haunt and to taunt. So maketh sure thy message is loud and clear.'

Dickhead and Bernardo waited guard at the entrance to the secret passage while Will and the king set off down the dingy corridor. They looked like three figures moving in single file along the narrow, winding passage. First, the king, then the king's shining bright dis-embodied head and, finally, Will, who was garbed all in black and with a soot-covered face.

The haunting trio had gone a distance of three hundred yards when the king stopped and indicated that they had reached the sliding panel door leading into Wolsey's room. He had to speak in a loud whisper to make himself heard above the thunderous snoring coming from the other side of the wall. ''Tis Wolsey's room,' he said. 'I shalt wait for the shriek before delivering my lines.'

Will nodded, quietly slid open the door and then slipped inside the bedroom with Henry's ghost head gleaming at his side. He tip-toed over to the four-poster bed and prodded the sleeping figure with the bottom of the pole holding the head.

'*Mein Gott in himmel!*' came the sudden shout as a rudely awakened Hans Holbein sat bolt upright in bed and found himself staring into the fluorescent face of King Henry.

From the other side of the wall came Henry's hollow-sounding voice. 'Cardinal Thomas Wolsey,' he shouted into the bucket. 'this is thy King Henry, the master whom thou swore to always obeyeth. Giveth thyself up to the guards this instant and demandeth that they throweth thee into the Tower for my murder. Confess thee to all thy sins, and avow that only the king's word is law in this merrie, green and pleasant land. And remembereth to thinketh and drinketh Thames Mead.'

There had been long and bitter argument before it was

agreed to add the final sentence. Dickhead won the day when he pointed out that Thames Mead would pay one hundred gold crowns for the sponsorship of the message.

Will rapidly retreated from beside Holbein's bed, and rejoined the king in the secret passage. 'Wrong room!' he hissed at Henry.

The king looked wildy about him, and then cussed. 'Drat my danglers,' he said. 'Of course. Wolsey did moveth to the larger bedroom opposite only last month.'

'Oh well,' whispered Will, ''tis as well to hath had a rehearsal. Poor Hans will thinketh he hath had a nightmare.'

They composed themselves alongside the sliding panel door leading to Wolsey's room. Then Will, Henry's head lighting the way, made his entrance on tiptoe. He crept over to the bed and prodded the sleeping figure with the pole.

'Bloody hell!' came the sudden shout as Daisy the chambermaid sat bolt upright and screamed so loudly that a startled Will dropped the pole holding Henry's head. Alongside her, Cardinal Wolsey came out of a deep sleep to see King Henry's head floating around the room as the unseen Will scrambled about trying to grab hold of the pole.

Wolsey's eyes were wide in terror as from the other side of the wall came Henry's hollow-sounding voice. 'Cardinal Thomas Wolsey,' he again shouted into the bucket. 'this is thy King Henry, the master whom thou swore to always obeyeth. Giveth thyself up to the guards this instant and demandeth that they throweth thee into the Tower for my murder. Confesseth thee to all thy sins, and avow that only the king's word is law in this merrie, green and pleasant land. And remembereth to thinketh and drinketh Thames Mead.'

As Will ducked out of the room, taking Henry's now under control head with him, two guards burst in brandishing swords.

'Taketh me into thy custody,' said a defeated and petrified Wolsey in a spiritless, monotonous voice. 'Throweth me into the Tower, and obeyeth only the king's laws. I hath murdered King Henry with mine own hand, and must now payeth for my sin.'

On the other side of the wall, Henry and Will gleefully shook hands. One down, one to go.

The bedroom of the Lord Chancellor, Thomas Cromwell, was two hundred yards further down the corridor. They paused outside the sliding panel door. 'Just a little quicker with thy delivery, thy Majesty,' whispered Will.

The king nodded, and held the bucket up to his face, ready to shout his lines.

Will slid back the door and, with Henry's head in tow, crept into the room. A lantern lit the far corner where Cromwell sat miserly counting hundreds of gold coins. He turned at the sound of Will bumping into the bed as he tried to retreat back to the corridor.

The Chancellor screamed in terror, his eyes fixed on the king's disembodied head floating before him.

From the other side of the wall came Henry's hollow-sounding voice. 'Thomas Cromwell, Lord Chancellor of all England,' he shouted into the bucket, 'this is thy King Henry, the master whom thou swore to always obeyeth. Giveth thyself up to the guards this instant and demandeth that they throweth thee into the Tower for my murder. Confess thee to all thy sins, and avow that only the king's word is law in this merrie, green and pleasant land. And remembereth to thinketh and drinketh Thames Mead.'

Cromwell, though nearly paralysed with fear, managed to reach for his sword and drew it from a sheath on his chair. He started slashing at the king's head, missing but slicing the thin pole to which it was tethered.

The pig-bladder head dropped to the floor, and as it bounced Will kicked out with an unseen foot and caught it on the half volley. Will, making the most of his skills as a noted street footballer, sent it up to the ceiling from which it rebounded to his soot-blackened head. It was, Will later reflected, quite a sight to see Henry's luminous, disembodied head bouncing around the Chancellor's bedroom. He balanced the bladder on his forehead and then dropped it down to his feet, and started juggling Henry's head from foot to foot, up on to his thigh and then down again to the feet. It was a masterful piece of control. Will then kicked it with all his might and the bladder scorched across the room and landed right in the region of, well, Cromwell's bladder. Henry's head had butted him in the balls.

As the Lord Chancellor folded in acute pain, Will retrieved the head and rejoined the king in the corridor just as the guards burst in.

'Taketh me from this place and giveth me the security of a Tower cell,' pleaded the Chancellor. 'I hath murdered the king, and now I hath to pay the price for

161

my sin. Locketh me away and obey only the commands of the king or his rightful successor.'

King Henry wanted to go for the hat-trick. 'Let us now frighten that frog woman back to France,' he said.

Too late. She had already gone.

When they got to her bedroom they found an empty bed, and a hand-written note that read: 'Now zat my beloved 'Enri hath drowned, I hath nuzzing to keepeth me here in zis shyte hole knowneth as England. I am off 'ome to wonderful France where zere is no talk of republicanism and where my lover Claude de Bedsop and I can settle down and lead a quiet life wizout all ze intrigue, plotting, conspiracies and bloody roast beef. If I 'ave anuzzer mouthful I will go quite mad. Please telleth Flirty of Flanders and Prince Porky zat zey are welcome to spend 'olidays wiz me in Cannes razzer zan shivering in Eastbourne; also tell Flirty zat her toe jobs hath done wonders for my love life. I 'ave even managed to convert Claude. I renounce all rights to ze English throne, and am just taking 'Enri's crown jewels zat I am entitled to as 'is widow. Oh oui, and I am also taking wiz me a signed confession of all 'Enri's sins zat I will 'ave published in ze French *Panorama de la Nouvelle* if anyone tries to snatch my jewels. Zat would not be a good zing for ze image of thy country and thy monarchy. *Au revoir Angleterre, et* good riddance!'

'And good riddance to thee, thou old bag,' said Henry as he finished reading the letter. 'She hath never had any rights to the English throne. She was a mere consort, and queen only in name. Shame that she tooketh my jewels, but if she tryeth to selleth them she will hath a sizable shock. They are mostly paste. The real jewels were soldeth years ago to help payeth for the building of St James's Palace.'

He re-read the line about his confession. 'What signed confession is she wittering on about?' he said. 'It must hath been something she gotteth me to sign while I wast the puppet of too much wine.'

He slapped Will on the back. 'This,' he said, holding up the farewell letter, 'is my passport to freedom. 'Tis evidence not only that she hath deserted me but also that she hath committed adultery with that woofter Claude de Bedsop. They are welcome to each other, whilst I am now all but free to marry my serving wench. It hath been a good night's work, Will.'

Will was not listening. He was kicking Henry's disembodied head in.

The journey back along the secret passage to Bernardo and Dickhead was not one that Will would ever like to repeat. The corridor seemed crammed with ghosts from Henry's past, and each of them carried their head underneath their arm. Will was too terrified to make identifications, but he recognised Anne Boleyn and Catherine Howard, and Sir Richard Empson and Edmund Dudley, two advisers to Henry's father whom he had sacrificed early in his reign as an unselfish sign of his repentance for Henry VII's excessive demands on the taxpayers.

Will tried frightening them off by bouncing Henry's disembodied head towards them, but it just went through them and they cackled with laughter.

Several of the ghosts tripped a fearful Henry with their clanking chains, and they pulled faces and jeered and booed him all the way along the corridor. 'Just wait until thou joineth us,' said Sir Richard from beneath his arm. 'Thou shalt payeth in spades for all the misery thou hath wrought.'

'We are doomed for ever to walk the night,' said Edmund Dudley, 'until thou hath joined the spirit world. While thee liveth we shalt haunt thee night after night. Thou thinkest thee can taketh life with an axe, but, nay, our spirits liveth on and this wilt be to thy cost.'

'Thou accuseth me, thy loyal wife, of witchcraft,' said Anne Boleyn. 'Thou knowest that not to be true, but now I hath become a witch and I shalt craft against thee until thou hath been paid for thy treachery.'

Francis Dereham, who had been executed along with Catherine Howard for his affair with the king's fifth wife, confronted Henry, thrusting himself before him with lewd movements of his transparent body. 'Recognise me, Henry old chap?' he said. 'Francis Dereham. Thou had me beheaded not because I was hathing my way with Catherine, but because thou knowest I could do it better than thee.'

He lifted his head and held it in front of Henry, and it laughed full in the king's face. 'And I still can,' he said mockingly. Then he and Catherine danced off together down the corridor.

Two large, laughing figures loomed in front of them. 'Thou hath triumphed, master,' said one.

'Long live the king,' shouted the other, adding 'oyez-oyez-oyez.'

These were not ghosts, but the living flesh of Bernardo and Dickhead.

The king and Will clasped each of them as if they had not seen them for years.

All the ghost images had disappeared as they reached the exit to the secret passage. Neither the king nor Will mentioned what they had seen, each preferring to think it must have been a figment of their imagination.

But Will knew by the perspiration leaking from the king's brow and the chalk-whiteness of his complexion that he had seen the same as he.

Will was glad that he was not in the king's Royal shoes. He did not have a ghost of a chance of beating the spirits.

The king was back on the throne within just hours of Wolsey and Cromwell being thrown into the Tower. Dickhead, confirmed as the king's new equerry and public relations officer, instructed the BBC to issue the following bulletin:

King Henry VIII lives! Long live the king. Tossed into the raging torrents of the River Thames by guards under the instruction of Cardinal Wolsey, His Majesty produced super-human strength and lung power to swim under water for an hour, so giving his enemies the impression that he had drowned. He beat off hungry sharks and sea monsters before reaching dry land down river. His Majesty then contacted his guards, all of whom remained steadfastly loyal to him, and – leading from the front, broadsword in hand – he

*commanded them to a rout of the knights who had
been bribed by Wolsey and Thomas Cromwell to
turn against the greatest king in the proud history
of this blessed country. After his great victory, King
Henry raised a glass of Thames Mead, and said,
"Tis good to be back in control of this green and
pleasant land. Let us, one and all, now hath a
merrie old time. As reward for the loyalty of my
subjects, I will raise taxes by only two instead of
four groats.' King Henry is now back on the
throne, and anybody who doubts it will hath his
head parted from his shoulders pretty damn quick.
Long live the king. This exclusive news bulletin
was brought to you by Thames Mead, the drink
that kings drink. Thinketh and drinketh Thames
Mead.*

Henry showed his gratitude to all those who had helped
him overcome Wolsey and Cromwell. He knighted
Charles Dickhead, gave Bernardo a palace of his own,
awarded the Reverend Downer a Bishopric, bought
Hans Holbein a new box of paints, and invited Will the
Quill to ask for anything that he wanted.

'Thou art not in a position to grant me the only thing
that I wish,' said Will.

The king gave a haughty laugh. 'Thou art speaking
to the King of the whole of England,' he said. 'I can do
or say anything I please. Name what it is that thou want
and it is thine. After all, without thee I would hath lost
my throne and also my head. Come on, Will. Do not be
shy. Just say it and it is thine.'

Will took a deep breath. 'All that I desireth is the hand in marriage of the serving wench, Nell Grinn,' he said.

'What?' roared the king. 'What? Is this thy idea of a jest? I think not much of it.'

'But that is my wish,' said Will. 'She is the woman, the only woman, that I love.'

Henry started striding around the Palace court room, steam coming from beneath his crown. There was a hint of a limp as he walked because his ulcerated leg was giving him gyp, and he was not in the best of moods despite his triumph.˙

'Thou hath asked the one thing that I cannot give,' he said. 'Nell Grinn hath stolen my heart.'

'But she stoleth mine first,' said Will. 'And she loveth me in return.'

'When the King of England maketh up his mind on the lady to whom he wisheth to be betrothed then that is it,' said Henry. 'Thy request is denied.'

Will risked his neck. 'But thou art hurting Nell as much as me,' he pleaded. 'We loveth each other. Thou art old enough to be her father, and cannot give her the happiness and contentment that I can...'

'Thou hath gone too far,' bellowed Henry, taking this as a challenge to his ability to satisfy a woman in bed. 'If thou had not done so much to save my throne, thy head wouldst be at my feet this second.'

˙For many years, King Henry suffered from ulcerated legs caused by his frequent falls from horses while out hunting. He was continually having to have the ulcers drained. In 1538 his draining ulcer had clogged, causing a clot of blood that brought a blockage of his lungs. Henry's face turned black, and for a week he was rendered speechless. His temper was short, and he would have heads off at a whim.

The king stopped walking, a gleam suddenly coming to his eye.

'I knowst how we can settle this,' he said, clapping his podgy hands together. 'How doth thou fancieth a duel?'

'A jewel?' said Will. 'Thou cannot buyeth me off with a mere bauble. That is no way to settle this issue of the heart.'

'Not a jewel,' barked Henry. 'A duel. Thee and me, on horseback against each other with lances. We shalt joust for Nell's fair hand.'

The true meaning of what the king was saying settled slowly on Will like a bad smell. 'But thou art famous as the greatest jouster in the whole of England,' said Will.

'England *and* Europe,' corrected the king, 'but I doth hath the handicap of a bad leg.'

'But I hath never jousted before in my life.'

'Thou must be jesting.'

'Nay, I hath never jousted.'

'And thou callest thyself an Englishman?' thundered the king. 'Every Englishman worth his salt hath to experience the thrill and the challenge of a charge. No more arguments. A duel it is.'

'But I hath only ever ridden a mule,' said Will.

'I wilt provide a charger,' said the king. 'And I cannot be fairer than this, I shalt also let you hath Bernardo to coach thee in the finer points of jousting. He informeth me that he was a fine jouster until losing his eye in a duel.'

Will's right eye winked rapidly at the thought of being jabbed with a lance.

'When doth the duel take place?' asked Will.

'One week of the morrow, at the Great Windsor Jousting Tournament,' said the king. 'I wanteth this matter settled quickly so that I can make Nell my wife next month.'

Will thought of Nell, her sweet face, her soft lips, her dazzling smile, her cute nose, her blue eyes, and her big knockers.

'Your challenge is accepted,' he heard himself saying. 'The duel is on.'

**Will the Winker
A portrait by
Hans Holbein**

I hath been gripped by this madness that
masquerades as a feeling called love.
What knoweth I of duels and jousts?
I am but a simple wordsmith.
My quill is my lance, and I would much
more confident be if the King had allowed
me to select the weapons.
A pen in my hand, I am an opponent fit
for any man, but I wouldst not give
a glance to a lance.
A duel, I fear, could come to mean adieu.

11

THE art of jousting had not featured prominently in Will the Quill's *The Compleat Historiae of Olde England*. He looked up his one reference to it that came in the chapter on King Arthur and his Knights of the Round Table. 'The joust,' he had written, 'was a mock battle between two horsemen charging at full gallop towards each other with levelled lances, each attempting to knock the other off. It was a sport enjoyed by King Arthur's Knights, apart from by those who suffered such minor injuries as broken backs, pierced bodies, snapped necks and the occasional fatal accident caused by a fall on to the head.'

Will was sitting in his garret the day after accepting the challenge of a duel from King Henry, and was quietly berating himself for his stupidity. 'Why,' he thought to himself, 'did I alloweth the king to dictateth the terms of the duel? I should have suggested something a little less dangerous such as a running race around Hampton Court, or a poetry contest. But to agreeth to a jousting duel was as ridiculous as King Alfred entering a cooking competition.'

He was going to be coached by Bernardo, who was hardly likely to give him tips on how to topple his beloved king off a horse in front of a cheering crowd at the annual Windsor Jousting Tournament. Will was just considering the easy option of throwing himself out of the garret window when his mood of despair was interrupted by a call on the yellyphone.

'Hello,' came a voice that sent a shiver down his back. ''Tis Nell 'ere. Is Will in?'

'I'm willing if thou art,' thought Will.

'Cometh on up,' Will shouted into his bucket. 'The door is openeth.'

Nell arrived four minutes later, her pleasantly enormous bosom heaving as she fought for breath after the haul up the twelve flights of stairs. It was her first visit to his abode, and doubtless her last.

'Stap me, Will,' she said, sinking on to the bucket seat and taking long pants of air, ''ow doth thou manage these stairs every day? Gawd, I feel as puffed as if I hath just served a regiment.'

Will waited for her to get her breath back, and then took it away again with a passionate kiss. She responded with what was something close to lust, and Will's quill was quivering as they rolled around on the floor. He expertly removed the girdle holding her six underskirts in place, and his hand was wandering to her nether regions when conscience got the better of him. With great reluctance, he pulled back and put his quill away.

'Art thou not going to nobbeth me, Will?' said a clearly disappointed Nell, her breath now coming in short pants.

''Tis not right that I taketh advantage of thee,' said Will. 'We must not knoweth each other in that manner until we are united in the eyes of the church. I loveth thee so much, Nell, that I wouldst die for thee.'

'Well you wilt, Will,' she said, 'if thou goeth through with this crazy duel. I overheardeth the king talking to his cronies at the bar last night and he sayeth he intendeth to breaketh thee into two.'

'Talk is cheapeth,' said Will, trying hard to disguise the fear that was lumping in his throat like a small boulder. 'The king is the most boastful man in the whole of England, and 'tis time that he was putteth in his place.'

Nell stood and cuddled him. 'Dear brave, courageous, daft-as-a-duck Will,' she said. 'I knoweth the king liketh to bloweth his own horn, but everybody sayeth that he is one of the finest horsemen and jousters in the land. How much jousting hath thou done?'

'Very little,' admitted Will. 'In fact I wouldst not know a lance if it hit me between the eyes.'

'So why risk thy life in this silly duel?'

'Because,' said Will, ''tis the only outside chance I hath of winning thy hand.'

'But thou must understand, Will, that my father wilt not allow me to marry thee regardless of the duel,' said Nell. ''Tis not that he does not like thee...'

'He hates me,' said Will.

'...'tis just that he wanteth what he considers the best for me, and he feeleth that thou cannot provideth what he wanteth for me.'

Nell looked around the cramped room. 'But thou seemeth to liveth well here,' she said. ''Tis nice and cosyeth and I just loveth the sackcloth curtains.'

''Tis only temporary,' said Will. 'I wouldst not expecteth thee to liveth here if we gotteth married. Once I getteth my England history book published, and my divorce finalised I wouldst getteth us a nice little two-bedroomed cottage in a quainteth olde English village, with roses growing around the door, a nice thick thatch

173

on the roof and a stateth of the art yellyphone.'

'The king hath offered me a wing of Hampton Court to myself,' said Nell. 'But I wouldst much rather liveth with thee in that cottage.'

She started to weep. 'But 'tis not to be, Will,' she said. 'My father hath banned me from seeing thee again, and he wouldst killeth me if he kneweth I were here visiting thee.'

'He would hath to let me marryeth thee if I winneth that duel,' said Will. 'Even the king wouldst expecteth it. He believeth in the chivalry of the great knights. If the winner of the duel is to hath thy hand then so be it.'

'But, Will,' said Nell, pearl-size tears welling in her beautiful blue eyes, 'thou cannot win, and I wouldst rather thou giveth up my hand and the duel rather than thy life.'

Will was about to reply to the effect that he did not wish to live without her when a voice sounded from between Nell's legs.

'Hello, is Will the Quill in?'

Nell's hands flew involuntarily to her face. 'Bloweth my behind!' she exclaimed. ''Tis my father. If 'e finds me 'ere I'm in for a goodeth 'iding.'

'Quickly,' said Will. 'Up on to the roof. Waiteth there until he hath gone.'

Nell scrambled on to Will's shoulders, and clambered through the hole that served as a window and on to the roof.

'Sorry to keep thee waiting,' Will shouted into the bucket. 'Who art thou?'

''Tis Lemmie Pulham, the Peacock and Partridge

174

innkeeper,' came the reply. 'Canst I talk to thee on a matter most urgent?'

'Cometh on up,' Will shouted. 'The door is openeth.'

Pulham climbed the twelve flights of stairs, and was panting like an overworked drayhorse when he finally arrived at the garret.

'Well knicketh me down and knockleth me,' he said through heavy breaths, 'if that ain't the steepest climb this side of Tower 'ill. If our Nell couldeth seeth 'ow thou liveth she wouldst soon losest 'er ardour for thee.'

Will indicated for Pulham to sit on the bucket seat, and noticed to his horror Nell's girdle on the floor beside it. He nonchantly picked up the girdle, and casually attached it around his waist.

'Excuseth me,' he said, his eye flickering at the speed of a bumble bee's wings. 'Thou hath caught me in a state of undress.'

Pulham watched him with a look of disdain. 'If our Nell couldeth see the way thou dresseth,' he said, 'she wouldst understand why I am opposeth to any bethrothel. A girdle, a winking eye and a too-pretty face. I knowst thy type. Bottom scavengers we calleth them in my neck of the woods. Well thou are not going to scavenge our Nell's bottom.'

'I hath never scavenged a bottom in my life,' said Will, dropping his voice down to his boots. 'My love for Nell is as pure as the driven snow. If all thou hath cometh here for is to harangueth me then I must asketh thou to leaveth, as thou didst me when I was last in thy alehouse.'

Pulham put up a hand. 'Wow, Will,' he said. 'Holdeth

thy horses. I am not here to talketh about Nell, but about the duel.'

'But that is all to do with Nell.'

'Fiddle faddle, foodidilly sticks,' said Pulham firmly. 'This duel could maketh me a fortune, Will, and I art ready to cut thee in on the action.'

He leaned forward in a conspiratorial manner. 'As thou no doubt knowest, I art a gambler of the first degree,' he said. 'I hath checked the odds on thy duel with the king, and he is one hundred to one on favourite to beateth thee in the best of three charges.'

'Best of three?' said Will, the eye movement going up a notch. 'But I thought it was one duel and away.'

'Dribble my drabble, doth thee know anything at all about jousting?'

'Not a lot.'

'Well, letteth me assure thee that thou fighteth the best of three mock battles.'

Will gulped.

'The only way a real gambler can maketh money on this one-sided match,' Pulham said, 'is to taketh a time-fall bet.'

'A time-fall bet?' said Will, who did not know a gamble from a ramble.

''Tis a bet in which thou not only hath to name the winner but the time in which he winneth, or, in your case, loseth.'

Will gave a timely nod of his head.

'Even the most novice of riders is expecteth to stayeth on his horse for thirty seconds in each charge,' said Pulham. 'The best odds are for somebody coming off in less than thirty seconds.'

Will wanted to say 'put your alehouse on it', but bit his tongue.

'What I am hereth for, Will,' the landlord said in his friendliest tone, 'is to asketh for thee to be off thy horse in under twenty seconds in each charge.'

'Thou art asking me to throweth the fight!' exclaimed an aghast Will.

Pulham laughed an alehouse laugh that barrelled around the tiny room. 'Not throweth,' he said. '*Falleth*. Thou wouldst be disqualified and thy knight's nuts knuckleth if thou were to throweth thyself off thy horse. Thou needst to falleth off in a most unquestionable manner.'

'But thou art asking me to be dishonest,' said Will. 'That wouldst be against the code of chivalry that the knights hath followed these last four hundred years.'

'Looketh at it like this,' said Pulham. 'There is as much chance of thou beating King Henry in a jousting duel as there is of ever a man flying across the ocean blue. So as thou art going to loseth anyway, why not do it quickly and earneth?'

'Earneth?' said Will.

'I wouldst get odds of twenty to one on thou losing in two straight falls inside a total of forty seconds,' said the calculating Pulham. 'By staking fifty golden coins, I wouldst win one thousand gold crowns. I wouldst very quietly, and without any dingling dongling, handest thee one hundred crowns for thyself.'

One hundred crowns. Will quickly worked it out that at his present earning power it would take him twenty years to amass that amount.

'But by losing the duel I wouldst also loseth the hand of Nell,' said Will.

The barrel-house laugh again. 'Gongly dongly, man,' said Pulham, 'faceth facts. Thou hath not a hopeth in hell of beating the king. He is bigger than thee, stronger than thee, certainly a better jouster than thee, will hath a faster, stronger horse than thee, and wilt be protecteth by the judges so that he cannot possibly loseth.'

'What meanest thou?' said Will, his brow furrowing. 'The judges are on his side?'

'But of course,' said Pulham. 'I overheareth the king talking in the inn last night, and the contest judges were with him. He made it clear that if by any mischance they were to scoreth a victory for thee their heads wouldst be off their shoulders quicker than they could say Sir Lancelot.'

'It looketh then as if I cannot win,' said Will.

'Drat me by the dragpots, that is what I hath been telling thee,' said Pulham.

Will stood and pulled himself up to his full five foot five inches. 'Placeth thy bet, Landlord,' he said, his right eye wide open. 'But putteth all thy money on me!'

Pulham laughed so much that he fell off the bucket.

'If thou winneth this duel,' he said, 'thou can hath not only Nell's hand but every limb and juicy bone that she possesseth.'

Will held out his hand. 'Let us shaketh on that, sire,' he said. 'And I reiterateth that thou shouldst put all thy money on me to win in two falls.'

There were tears of laughter rolling down Pulham's

cheeks as he left. 'Thou art a true clunelly clum clown,' he said. 'I shalt be at Windsor to picketh thee up.'

Will put his thumbs inside his girdle, and puffed out his chest in a defiant stance. 'We shalt see,' he said. 'Methinks thou art in for the shock of the century.'

He helped Nell down through the roof window, and felt how enchanting she looked despite the pigeon droppings adorning her hair and dress.

'I heardeth every word,' she said. 'Thou should hath agreed to my father's offer on the time bet. At least thou would then hath had the consolation of makingeth a gain from thy pain.'

He kissed her sweet lips. 'Hath faith in me, fair Nell,' he said. 'Thy hand will be mine cometh the great tournament.'

'Now,' Will thought to himself, 'all I have to do is learneth to joust.'

Will had read all there was to read about jousting by the time he met up with Bernardo on Blackheath Common for his first lesson. He discovered that it was first introduced to England in the twelfth century by Richard the Lionheart as a way of keeping his resting soldiers fired up between the holy wars. In the earliest versions, some five hundred knights would be divided into two teams and, on a signal from the Earl Marshal and Knight Marshal, they would charge at each other with raised lances and swinging swords. It was supposed to have been sport, but such was the rivalry and spite out on the field that some of the finest soldiers in the land were being killed or seriously wounded. To cut the losses, a new two-man duel was devised, and to make it safer, in the fourteenth century, a tilt was introduced – a dividing barrier between the two confronting riders. It was now a controlled sport, but fatal injuries were still commonplace.

A points system was introduced, with four points for the knight whose lance struck his opponent's shield. But the true knight went for the 'kill', aiming to knock the other horseman off. Will read Sir Lancelot's guide to jousting, *Joust for Fun*, that he picked up for two groats at a bookstall in the Sunday market at Pudding Lane. 'Jousting,' wrote Sir Lancelot, 'is the art of getting thy lance into thy opponent's throat without him getting his lance within the span of a gnat's wing of thee. First thou must learn full control of thy horse at speeds of up to forty miles an hour, making sure to master how to maketh thy horse rear while retaining command of thy lance. Thy shield, steel enforced, should be strapped to thy left arm whilst thou couch the twelve-foot sharpened lance in thy right. The best-dressed mediaeval knight weareth a highly-polished armoured breast plate, closely-linked chain mail suit, and a plumed helmet displaying the colours of his sponsor, or perhaps that of his true love locked in a chastity belt some place awaiting his victorious return. The secret of winning at jousting is...'

And that was where the book ended. The rest of the pages had been torn out, and now Will knew why he had been able to buy it so cheaply. But at least he would be able to call on the vast knowledge of Bernardo, whose tales of his jousting duels had warmed up many a cold winter's evening at the Peacock and Partridge.

Will had read how jousting horses had been imported all the way from Eastern Europe by King Henry. These had the vast neck and short, broad back best suited to jousting. He looked forward to getting acquainted with his mount on Blackheath Common.

His disappointment could be measured in fathoms when Bernardo arrived with what could be best described, in all charity, as an old plodder. 'This is Goliath,' said Bernardo. 'He cometh with the king's compliments.'

'But 'tis a knackered old plough horse,' said Will, covering Goliath's ears so that he could not hear what was a fitting, though not flattering description. 'He hath been involveth in as many jousting tournaments as I hath, precisely none. What doth the king thinketh he is playing at?'

'A confidential word in thy ear, Will,' said Bernardo. 'Do not expecteth any favours from the king when it comes to any sporting match. Lead is slipped into the shoes of anybody playing him at tennis, and anybody challenging him to a wrestling match hast first to hath one hand tied behind his back. 'Tis why he is the unbeaten wrestling champion of all England.'

The good thing about learning to ride on Goliath was there was no danger of Will being thrown. At full gallop he went no faster than five miles an hour, and Will only fell off six times while learning balance and getting the sort of co-ordination with his mount that was all-important for a jouster. It has to be admitted, however, that Will did consider it quite embarrassing to find himself being overtaken by ambling lovers and nannies with children strolling across the common.

After three hours he was satisfied that he had conquered the riding side. 'Now, Bernardo,' he said, 'where art my shield and my lance?'

Bernardo looked embarrassed, and rightly so, when he produced a cardboard shield and long broom handle.

'What are these?' said an astonished Will.

''Tis thy shield and lance,' said Bernardo.

''Tis not a shield and lance,' said Will. ''Tis a piece of cardboard and a broom handle.'

''Tis all thou can practice with until the day of the tournament,' said Bernardo. 'The king hath made it abundantly clear that nobody must lendeth thee a shield and lance. He feeleth it would giveth thee an unfair advantage if thou rehearseth with a lance before the duel.'

It was beginning to dawn on Will that the odds were stacked against him.

He climbed aboard Goliath after giving him an hour's rest. 'Right, Bernardo,' he said, 'now what advice hath thou got for me? What tactics doth thou suggest I adopt?'

Will looked down from his vantage point on Goliath's back. Bernardo was peering down at his feet.

'I hath never jousted in my life,' he confessed, his glass eye lowered in shame.

'Thou what?' said Will, his suddenly raised voice causing Goliath to rear and toss him to the ground.

'Please keepeth this to thyself,' pleaded Bernardo. 'It wouldst finish me in the new society into which I hath moved if it were known that I hath been lying all these years about my past.'

'I doth not care two groats about thy past,' said Will. 'All I careth about is my future. Art thou telling me that thou knowst even less about jousting than I?'

Bernardo nodded. 'All I knoweth is that thou holdeth the lance and then gallopeth like mad towards thy opponent,' he said. 'But no matter if thou hath the most knowledgeable jouster in the whole of England to coacheth thee, thou will not be allowed to beat the king. He hath never been beaten in a jousting match in his life, and he could not possibly alloweth thee to taketh away his undefeated record.'

Will was nothing if not determined and resolute. Despite all the handicaps put in his way, he spent the next five days working out his own tactics while galloping – well, cantering – across Blackheath Common on Goliath. He placed a life size cut out of King Henry at a distance one hundred yards away, and continually charged at it with his broom handle raised and his cardboard shield gripped in his left hand. By the end of the week he was hitting the target at least once in every six charges.

Will was as ready as he ever would be.

The *Panorama Times*, now retitled *Hurrah Henry* (sponsored by Thames Mead), produced an eight-page supplement on the duel, with illustrations by Hans Holbein and a tale-of-the-tape and in-depth features. There were eighty-eight paragraphs describing the round-Europe battle triumphs of Henry, and another sixty paragraphs on Henry's unbeaten jousting career.

At the bottom of page eight there was one line on Will that he cut out and pasted into his scrapbook. It read: 'The opponent this afternoon is Will the Quill.'

Celebrities of the day gave their predictions:

Archbishop of Canterbury: 'I thinketh and prayeth that the king will winneth inside two minutes.'

Thomas Audley, first Speaker of the Reformation Parliament: 'Order! Order! The king will winneth by two falls to nil.'

Princess Christina of Milan, a prospective future wife for King Henry: 'Whata bellissimo calvesa the kinga doth hatha. He is a certain winner and willa shuduppa da facea of his opponent in three minutos.'

Sir Noel Lynes, the distinguished actor and stage manager: 'Methinks this is much ado about nothing but a grand triumph for our sovereign King Henry VIII.'

Dr Ivan O'Deah, the eminent physician recently released from the Tower: 'His Majesty the king is in the best of health and wilt disheth out the medicine to his opponent.'

Lord Kiljoy, the Lord Chief Justice: 'The king wilt winneth easily or there is no justice.'

Erasmus, the Dutch philosopher from Rotterdam: 'The king'll do 'im in two, and will be over the Moon, Brian.'

Sir Brian d'Klein, court minstrel and virginals virtuoso: 'His Majesty is nicely in tune for a well-orchestrated performance, and shalt conduct himself to a resounding victory.'

Will read through the supplement with growing dismay over the extent to which Charles – now Sir Charles – Dickhead had gone over to the Establishment.

This was how he started his preview of the duel:

The scene is set in the grounds of Windsor Castle this afternoon for one of King Henry's greatest triumphs in a career during which he hath proved himself indisputably the world's greatest jouster. Where art there anybody who can matcheth his strength, his speed, his horsemanship, his lancemanship, his shieldsmanship, his swordsmanship and allroundmanship? He today faceth an opponent of vast experience, a jouster extraordinaire who hath fought and won battles galore on the international jousting circuit, who is undoubtedly the number one contender for the title of World's Greatest Jouster. But our brave and courageous king is prepareth to put his undefeated record at risk so that his subjects can enjoy the sight of seeing him in action, and not being aloof as hath been the custom with many of his predecessors to the English throne which he graces with such style and splendour. The king putteth much of his success down to Thames Mead, the drink he taketh before retiring to bed every night and again each morning. His Majesty told Hurrah Henry exclusively, 'Remember, Thames Mead. Thinketh it, drinketh it.'

Will folded up the magazine and placed it inside his doublet. He sighed with nostalgia for the days when the *Times* was a voice against the king and his rotten regime. Now he felt part of it, even though he was

185

about to try to floor the man who modestly described himself as 'the greatest king in the whole of history.'

There was a joyous festive spirit in the grounds of Windsor Castle for the Great Annual Windsor Jousting Tournament. Huge colourful banqueting tents had been set up, decorated with hangings of tapestry and embroidered cloth. There were live displays of falconry, tumblers, fair amusements, archery contests, wrestling matches, sword fencing, boot throwing, Morris dancing, minstrels, jesters, jugglers, and, of course, jousters.

Will felt a tingle of excitement up his spine mixed with nervous tension as he watched the experienced knights jousting for the title of the Golden Lance of Windsor. He felt he had learned more from watching them for three hours than throughout his week on Blackheath Common. What he learned above all else was that he had not the first or last idea about how to joust. They rode like men born to the saddle, and at speeds that made them a blur to even his wide-open left eye. Their lances were used as spears of destruction, and it was like the sound of thunder when they crashed them against the shields of their opponents. There were only two fatal accidents during their twenty-contest competition, although it was expected that several of the fallers would never walk again.

The climax of the tournament was to be Will's duel with the king, who witnessed all the action from his royal box in front of the jousting pitch. His Majesty was surrounded by dignitaries, and he was clearly at ease

186

and enjoying himself as he wolfed his way through three chickens, washed down with bottle after bottle of best French wine.

Will noticed that Sir Charles Dickhead was at the king's side getting stuck into the wine, along with the rehabilitated Dr Ivan O'Deah and his wife, who had talked Henry into releasing the mad doctor from the Tower. Nell was also in the box, looking a Hans Holbein picture in a hoop-skirted blue gown that was cut deep, showing off her prize assets. Today, the whole of her was the prize. She blew Will a kiss from behind the king's back, and wiped a tear away from her eye with a lace handkerchief, one of ten dozen that the king had given her after a trip to Paris.

Just as Will was lulling himself into thinking that the king would be too drunk to see let alone duel, Bernardo – acting as his second – brought him down to earth. 'His Majesty doth not like to duel on an empty stomach,' he reported, like a harbinger of doom. 'He sayeth that food and wine doth give him the energy necessary for a peak jousting performance.'

Will nodded in understanding as he nibbled on the dry biscuit and supped the water that had been left in his tiny changing room that he shared with a troupe of acrobats, a bearded lady, a fire-eating goat and a tribe of pygmies.

Bernardo helped Will dress for battle, although he felt as if he might have been better off dressing himself when Bernardo managed to put his breastplate on back to front and strapped the shield to his leg instead of his arm. It was the first time that Will had worn armour in his life, and he could not believe the weight of it. It must have weighed nearly one hundred weight, and when the shield was eventually strapped to his left arm he felt as if it was going to be pulled out of its socket. His plumed helmet must have been worn previously by a colossus. It swamped Will's head, and when the visor was dropped he could hardly see a thing and could hear even less.

Bernardo opened the visor and called inside that it was time to mount Goliath. His horse was looking as good as it had ever done, decorated in a bit of old curtaining that dangled down by his huge hooves and with a saddle that had probably been used in the first year of the hundred years war.

It took Bernardo and the entire tribe of pygmies to lift Will into the saddle. His lance was handed up to him, and – compared with the weight of the broom handle with which he had been practising all week – it felt as if he had a stone pillar resting on his arm.

Will saw through his still-open visor King Henry looking, well, like Henry the Magnificent about to mount his charger that was dressed in crimson velvet, with trappings of gold embroidered with the initial 'K' and the king's motto *Coure Loyall* (True Heart). He noticed all his sycophantic followers lining up to wish him well. The king blew a kiss and bowed in the direction of Nell, and was then given what seemed to be a whispered message of good luck by Dr O'Deah's wife. The king beckoned Lemmie Pulham, called out something about placing a bet and then, for Will, it all went black. His visor had dropped into place. Bernardo gave Goliath a slap on the rump, and battle commenced.

Will was aware that he was galloping, but in which direction he knew not. Goliath had become startled by the roar of the crowd, and he was off and running like the wind.

Even with his visor down, Will could hear the crowd going wild in their support for the king. His lance suddenly felt as if it had hit a wall, and the cheers in his ears turned to loud groans.

Goliath had come voluntarily to a halt, and Will pulled up his visor to get his bearings. The jousting track was now directly behind him, and he looked back to see the amazing sight of the king stretched out alongside his horse. He was being attended to on the ground by, among others, Dr O'Deah and Sir Charles Dickhead.

Will trotted back to where he had left Bernardo, and as he passed the royal box Nell was up on her feet shouting above the buzz of a stunned crowd. 'Goeth for it, Will!' she yelled. 'Thou art one fall from winning my hand.'

'What happened?' he said to Bernardo.

'Thou scored a perfect hit, that is what happened,' said a bemused Bernardo. 'Even my crystal eye could not hath forseen that. The king toppled. We'll all pay for this. Goeth easy with him, Will. Thinketh of his pride, and thinketh of our necks.'

The king greedily drank down a bottle of brandy before the second round, purely for medicinal purposes of course. His attendants placed him back in the saddle and round two of the duel commenced before Will had time to drop his visor.

Bernardo gave Goliath a slap, and the roar of the

189

crowd set him off on another terrified gallop. This time Will was able to see that they were heading directly for the king, whose lance was raised and pointing towards Will's throat. They were the required five feet apart because of the dividing barrier between them. Will lifted his lance and, with his eyes closed tight, made a wild lunge. There was a loud thump of a noise as the tip of his lance smashed into the king's shield. The impact knocked His Majesty backwards and, losing control of his horse, he fell sideways on to the ground.

The king of jousting was dead. Long live the king.

Will was carried shoulder high in triumph to the royal box by the knights who had been competing in the Golden Lance tournament. He went down on one knee in front of Nell and, with Lemmie Pulham looking on approvingly, made a public proposal. 'Canst I hath thy hand in marriage, pretty maiden,' he said, hastily adding, 'once I am free of my first wife.'

'Though mayst,' came the roared reply, not from Nell but from King Henry who was in surprisingly good spirits considering that he had just lost his undefeated jousting record.

Henry, winking across at Pulham, made an announcement to the gathered throng. ' I doth not wish it to go into the record books that my unbeaten record was taken by a commoner,' he said. 'From this day forth Will here shalt be known as the Duke of Wapping, and his bride to be as the Duchess. What is more, I shall start them on their way to married life with a gift of one thousand gold coins.'

The shock of it all cured Will's wink, and he

immediately became a converted royalist. He looked forward to converting the virgin Nell at the first opportunity.

Much later that day, at a banquet to celebrate the tournament and the duel, King Henry took Will on one side during the dancing.

'Thou seeth that old frump dancing over there,' he said, pointing to Mrs O'Deah, the doctor's wife.

Will nodded his head.

'Well twenty-two years ago she looked as good, if not better, than the lovely Nell,' he said. 'I could not resist getting my royal leg over, and only today, just before our duel, did she reveal to me that the beautiful Nell is, in fact, my daughter.'

'Drat my danglers,' said Will.

'We will keep it a secret between thee and me,' he said. 'If thou breathe a word of it I shall hath thy head off.'

'So I did not beat thee fair and square in the duel?'

The king gave a barrel-house laugh. 'As if thou could hath done,' he said. 'I remaineth the greatest jouster in the whole of England,' he said. 'Oh yes, and also the richest. Sir Lemmie Pulham and I got odds of one hundred to one on thee winning.'

It was King Henry's turn to wink. 'Now thou must excuseth me,' he said. His eye had fallen on the comely Catherine Parr.

Will decided that he had a new title for the king's book: *Carry On, Henry*.